HIGH LIE

A MIAMI JONES CASE

AJ Stewart

Jacaranda Drive Publishing

Los Angeles, California

www.jacarandadrive.com

Cover artwork by Streetlight Graphics

ISBN-10: 0985945559

ISBN-13: 978-0-9859455-5-8

Books by AJ Stewart

Stiff Arm Steal
Offside Trap
High Lie
Dead Fast
Crash Tack

For Heather and Evan, my muse and my mirror.

Thanks to Andrew Weatherston for all the reading, and for being there all these years, even when we are thousands of miles apart.

CHAPTER ONE

"The kid was dead for all money."

I listened to Lucas but didn't take my eyes from the boy. He was small, like he never had a proper meal in his life, and his skin, tanned brown across his shoulders, was a sickly yellow color in his face.

"The buggers wrapped him up in a carpet and tossed him overboard," continued Lucas, in his broad Australian drawl.

I pulled an old sweatshirt with an Oakland A's logo on it over the boy's head. It wasn't cold inside my house, with both front and back doors open, letting the breeze drift through at will, but the boy had the twin ailments of mild hypothermia and shock. He stared into middle distance as

I pulled the sleeves into place, his heavy eyebrows twitching.

"What is your name?" I asked him.

"I been talking to him since I fished him out of the drink," said Lucas. "English, Spanish, even threw a bit of Chinese at him. Not a peep out of him."

I stood and turned to Lucas.

"You speak Chinese?"

"A bit. G'day, g'bye, thanks. I can order a beer. We get a few well-to-do Chinese chartering the big yachts at the marina."

Danielle wandered in from the kitchen with a cup of tea for the kid. Her brown hair was mussed, but it looked as if she had paid a hundred bucks to get it that way, rather than having been woken up at 2 a.m. by a fist banging on our door. She handed the tea to the boy and he took it as if grasping the Holy Grail.

"Where was this, again?" I asked, wiping my face. My hair was also a mess, but on me it looked like I'd just crawled out of bed.

"Jupiter. The inlet. Two fellas launched a tinny out of DuBois Park and puttered out about a half mile."

"You were out at sea?"

"Me? Nah, I was in the river. These fellas had clearly been drinking, and I thought they might get themselves in a spot of bother."

Danielle looked up at Lucas.

"What were you doing in the Loxahatchee River at one in the morning?" she asked.

Lucas smiled. He was tanned like a cowhide, his sandy hair sun-bleached, his limbs lean but powerful. The net effect was an ageless look, not young but indeterminably old, and his smile was that of a mischievous ten-year-old boy.

"Certainly not crabbing, Deputy. That would be illegal."

Danielle shook her head and returned her attention to the boy.

"So you followed them out?" I said.

"Yeah. Like I say, they were having a bit of trouble keeping their boat in a straight line, so I followed 'em. Just beyond the drop-off they stopped. Seemed like an odd place to fish in the dead of night, so I circled around and cut my engine."

"And?"

"They nearly tipped their boat over more than once, trying to get whatever it was out. Not too many things are dead weight like that, so I got a bit suss."

The boy sipped the tea, the first time he had moved of his own accord since Lucas had arrived at my doorstep with the kid in his arms.

"So what happened?"

"They managed to dump their cargo, then they scarpered real quick. I was only about ten feet away by that stage—hiding in the moon shadow, you could say— and I figured they weren't dumping nuclear waste, so I grabbed a tank and jumped in."

"Why did you have a scuba tank?" Danielle asked.

"Night photography." He smiled again. "I do a bit of underwater night photography."

No one was buying that story, but Lucas wasn't working too hard to sell it.

"So anyways, I jump in, flick on my light, and catch a rolled-up carpet sinking toward the bottom."

"Wasn't it heavy?" I said.

"Yep. We didn't stop going down, but the air trapped inside the rug made it a slow drop. I cut the twine they'd used to tie it up, and let the thing unravel. Thought I knew what it was, but I was still surprised when I seen that little fella tumble out."

We all looked at the boy for a moment. He glanced at Lucas, then refocused on the mug of tea.

"I can't believe he didn't drown," Danielle said.

"He was lucky, that's for sure," said Lucas. "Lucky they knocked him out. There's a little cut on the side of his head you might wanna take a look at," he said, pointing at the boy. "He was unconscious, so he didn't panic, didn't suck in a lot of water. He bounced back pretty quick once I got him in the ducky and gave him a shot of mouth-to-mouth."

Danielle took a look at the boy's head, then stood and walked to the bathroom.

Lucas leaned into me.

"Sorry, mate, hope I didn't interrupt anything with the wife," he said, winking.

"It's two in the morning, Lucas. Trust me, it's fine. And she's my girlfriend, not my wife. You know that."

He smiled. "Why is that?"

I just shook my head.

Danielle came back with a first-aid kit, and the boy allowed her to put some antiseptic cream on his head, then wrap it in a bandage. Then she took the tea from him and placed her soft hands over his. It was a nurturing gesture and I saw the boy physically relax.

"Do you speak English?" she asked. "*Hablas inglés?*"

The boy's face showed no emotion, but he whispered, "*Si.* Yes." The first noise he'd made.

Danielle gave the boy a soft smile. It was the same look that lifted the weight of the world from my shoulders, but I had seen it only sparingly of late.

"What is your name?"

"Desi," said the boy.

She nodded and took this in. "It's nice to meet you, Desi. I'm Danielle. This man here is called Miami, and the man who pulled you from the water is Lucas."

The boy looked at us and we nodded to him. Still no smile, but at least eye contact.

"How old are you, Desi?" continued Danielle.

"Eleven."

Danielle nodded and I thought how glad I was she was there. I was pretty certain the kid would have clammed up for Lucas and me, even if we'd offered him a trip to Disney World.

"Now Desi, you are safe here. We can help you. You are not in trouble." She rubbed her fingers along his hands, then continued.

"Who were those men, Desi?"

The boy looked down, perhaps unsure. I couldn't read his face at all.

"It's okay, Desi," said Danielle, "but it is important."

The boy didn't look up, not for a time, as if considering whether or not he could trust us. I could hardly blame him for that. If someone had rolled me in a carpet and tossed me in the Atlantic, I'd be reconsidering my trust parameters as well. But the kid must have come to some sort of decision, because he looked at her and sighed.

"Bad men," he said.

"Yes, bad men." Danielle nodded. "But who were they, Desi?"

The boy hesitated again, then frowned. "They took my money."

Now it was Danielle's turn to frown. "Your money? Did you know these men?"

The boy nodded slowly. "Si."

"Where did you know them from, Desi?"

The kid hesitated again, but came to a decision quicker this time. Danielle had a face a guy could trust, and it seemed the boy did.

"At the *fronton*."

"Fronton?" said Danielle. Desi nodded. She turned to us with a question on her face.

Lucas frowned at me. "What's a fronton?" he asked.

"It's like a giant squash court. It's where they play *jai alai*."

"High lie?"

"Yeah, jai alai. It's a sport. Spanish, I think. It was popular in South Florida back when Don Johnson was somebody."

I got down on my haunches so I was at eye level with the boy.

"The fronton? Where they play jai alai?" I said.

Desi nodded.

"Which fronton?" I said. This time I got no reaction, and the boy looked to Danielle. So did I.

"Fort Pierce, West Palm Beach, or Dania?" she said.

"Palm Beach," said Desi.

I stood and looked at Lucas.

"The casino is taking bets from an eleven-year-old kid?" Lucas asked.

"How much money did you owe?" said Danielle.

"Two hundred," said Desi.

"They dumped him in the drink for two hundred bucks?" said Lucas.

"They took two hundred dollars from you?" asked Danielle.

Desi shook his little head slowly.

"They take four hundred. Money for my papa."

We all traded glances, then Danielle turned back to the boy. "Where is your papa, Desi?"

Desi looked at the floor, avoiding eye contact with Danielle. "Cuba," he said.

Lucas and I retreated to bar stools at the kitchen counter, and I made coffee. We let the professional talk to the boy. Danielle sat on the sofa and chatted with him. We learned that the boy was placing bets with two big men, one with no hair, the other with hair of fire.

"Hair of fire?" said Danielle.

"*Rojo*," said Desi.

Danielle sat with the boy until he finished his tea and the life seeped back into him. Then she got up and came into the kitchen.

"I've got the morning shift, so I might as well go in early, see if I can find out anything about these guys."

She went to shower and change, and I asked Desi if he wanted anything to eat, to which I got no response. When Danielle came out she was in her green sheriff's uniform, which earned a look of concern from Desi.

"It's okay," she said. "You are safe here. You're not in trouble. I'm a sheriff's deputy, you understand? *Policia?* I can help you." The boy watched her without expression.

"These men here," she said, looking up at Lucas and me, "they can help you, too. You stay here, and we will help you."

The boy nodded.

Danielle grabbed her keys and kissed me. "See if you can get him to eat something. If I find anything, I'll call you."

Danielle headed out, and I made a ham sandwich and placed it and a glass of ice water in front of Desi. He didn't speak but his eyelids looked heavy. I knew that feeling. Not just 2 a.m. speaking. The adrenaline of almost being drowned had worn off, and fatigue was setting in fast. I'd been in my fair share of high-stress situations, and I knew the drop after an adrenaline rush was like a cliff. I grabbed a blanket and a pillow and brought them to the sofa.

"Sleep, *siesta*?" I said.

Desi nodded, his head almost unable to hold itself erect. I dropped the pillow on the sofa and he fell back into it, then I placed the blanket over him. He looked up at me through heavy eyes, as if studying me.

"Sleep," I said, and he did.

Lucas and I took our coffee out onto the patio. The lights from Riviera Beach twinkled across the Intracoastal, and we sat on the loungers for a while, watching the city sleep. A cool breeze brushed my skin, as it did in the season. Lucas broke the silence.

"Some yobbos were going to kill that boy for a measly two hundred."

I nodded in the darkness. That fact had been gnawing at me since I had heard it. "Yobbo?" I said.

"Yeah, yobbo. Dunderhead, goose, moron."

Talking with Lucas was like learning a new language.

"Something needs to be done about that," he said.

I nodded again.

"What time does that casino open?" he said.

"In the morning I guess, but I think the jai alai starts at around lunchtime."

Lucas said nothing in return.

"You thinking we should pay a visit?" I said.

"This is not something you need get involved with."

"There's a half-drowned Cuban boy marooned on my sofa. I'm involved."

"Sorry about that, mate."

"Don't be. You saved that boy's life. The least I can do is find out why you had to."

Lucas sat up in his lounger but didn't take his gaze from the dark water. "Lunchtime, you reckon?"

"Yeah."

"That a hammock over there, between them palms?"

"Yes."

"Mind if I borrow it for a bit?"

"Lucas, I have a spare room. You can get some sleep inside." It occurred to me that Lucas was probably coming down off a pretty significant adrenaline high himself.

"That's okay, I prefer sleeping outside."

"What about the bugs?" I said. The breeze off the water kept the bugs manageable most evenings, but if the wind dropped during the night the hammock could end up looking like a wheat field during a locust plague.

"I don't bother the bugs, the bugs don't bother me."

He got up and wandered over to the hammock, sliding into it with the practiced style of a submariner. Within a minute, he was snoring. I took that as my cue. I slipped back inside and locked the front door, then checked on Desi. He hadn't moved a muscle. He looked peaceful, which I considered a fair effort for a kid who had been rolled up in a carpet and tossed in the ocean only a few hours earlier. I padded to Danielle's and my bedroom but left the door open, and I flopped onto the bed for a few Z's. I pushed thoughts of Desi hitting the water from my mind, only to have them replaced by the feeling that a long night was likely to turn into an even longer day.

CHAPTER TWO

The West Palm Beach Casino and Jai Alai sat on the good side of I-95, across from Palm Beach International Airport. It was an older establishment that had seen its heyday about the same time as Elvis. Big seventies-style retro letters proclaimed the name of the place across the windowless facade, and as I parked my Ford Escape in the spacious and near-empty lot, the thought occurred that the signage wasn't so much seventies retro as seventies original.

Inside, the casino was like a cave. In Vegas they lit their places like it was always close to midnight, but here the ambience was more one of power failure. A few fluorescent tubes threw dull light across mostly empty card tables. The carpet was black with colored flecks in it, and it held the latent stench of years of cigarette smoke despite the venue now being allegedly smoke-free.

We wandered past a bored-looking woman at the information and cash kiosk and turned toward a sign that read *Jai Alai*. Through the door was another world. A cavernous space with high ceilings—on one side twenty rows of seats that were as sparsely populated as the card tables; on the other a brightly lit court the width of a half-dozen bowling alleys and twice as long. One long side was exposed to the seating behind a net, with all the other sides painted Wimbledon green. Two men dressed like polo players were on the hardwood floor of the court and two men in referee's stripes stood just off the playing area. Everyone wore beaten helmets that also looked like remnants of the seventies.

Lucas and I stood for a moment, taking in the game. There were two players. Each wore a long scoop on his right hand that doubled his reach. One player used the scoop to slingshot a white ball at the far wall. When it bounced back the other player used his scoop to catch the ball, then slung it back at the wall again. Each player did this with considerable force until the ball seemed to bounce away from one player, at which point an announcer's voice rocked across the loudspeakers.

"Point for Roto. Roto two. Next is Miguel."

It must have been the end of the game because the defeated player left the court and was replaced by another. Oddly, he wore a shirt with the number twenty-five on the back but the number four on the front. We took the lapse in play to scour the crowd. It wasn't a big job. The place might have held four hundred seats but only about thirty of them were taken, and as I scanned the room I noted that most of those were not paying a lot of attention to the game.

"There," said Lucas, slapping my shoulder.

In the back row, under the shadow of a darkened, corporate box-type structure, sat two big guys. They were both pale, and wearing tank tops to show off muscles that would have been impressive a decade earlier. Everyone else in the room was either Cuban or Latino, so the two white guys looked positively albino. One had a shining bald head, shaved as close as his chest, and the other had his hair close-cropped, like a marine. His hair was red. Rojo. Hair of fire.

Lucas and I had left Desi in my house with food and water and directions to get some more sleep. I told him we would be back in a couple of hours, and I felt a little bad that I didn't own a television for him to watch. He hadn't given us anything new to work with, other than repeating the descriptions of the two big guys.

The descriptions sure matched the two lugnuts we stood in front of now. They were pale and bloated and wore the red eyes of a hangover. We crept along the second-to-last row and stood between them and the jai alai. It served its purpose and caught their attention.

"If you wanna black eye, you just stay right where you ah," said Baldy, in a thick Boston accent. That explained the sickly skin tone. Boston Irish didn't tan in the sun; they just turned the color of their beloved lobsters.

"I hear you boys are the ones to speak to about a little action," said Lucas, and for the first time I noticed how similar his accent was to that of the Bostonians. Maybe there were a lot of Irishmen in Australia, too. I had no idea.

"What action?" asked Baldy.

Lucas nodded toward the game, which had resumed with the echoes of the ball cracking off the walls.

"Jai alai," said Lucas.

"High lie?" said Redhead. "You mean the jay a-lay."

"It's generally pronounced *high lie*," I said.

Redhead shot me the same glance I bet he'd given every teacher since kindergarten, then looked back at the court. "Get lost," he said.

"Sorry, Blue," said Lucas. "My mistake. I guess you aren't the movers and shakers we heard about."

"You can lay bets in the casino," said Baldy.

"Yeah, that's not our kind of action," said Lucas.

"Or our kind of credit," I added.

Redhead eyed us both in turn.

"You guys cops?"

I was a former professional baseball player turned PI, and Lucas managed the high-end marina in Miami Beach, before which he had been in some kind of special forces doing who knew what for various governments and agencies. We might have had cop-like backgrounds, but we looked like a couple of past-their-prime beach bums searching for one last wave.

"No," I said. "We're not cops."

Redhead leaned back in his chair. "We had to ask, you know. Just in case you was wearing a wah."

A wire, indeed. I nodded and smiled as if it was a genius move, and Redhead clearly had every base covered. But the smile wasn't for his genius. It always amused me when these morons got their experience from TV. In real life, undercover cops were permitted to lie their asses off. Getting a cop to lie about being a cop wasn't grounds for anything, entrapment or otherwise. The concept of being undercover really didn't work if they could be found out by having to fess up the truth. Oh, you got me, I *am* a cop.

Redhead was evidently satisfied with his genius, however, because he stood slowly, trying to keep his head level. "Let's talk outside."

Both of the Irishmen put on shades to shield them from the midday sun. They bobbled when they walked, and I noted they both had thighs that would have done a Tour de France rider proud. But their muscled legs made it hard to walk, so I wondered what the objective was. They led us behind the main building, so the jai alai court was through the cinder block wall by us. On the other side was a mass of hedge and mangrove, and we could hear the roar of the freeway beyond.

"So how does this work, Blue? You take bets right outside the building?" said Lucas.

Redhead frowned at him as if he was learning the language. "No. We talk terms. If we like what we hear, we make a call."

Lucas nodded. "So what can you offer?"

"What you wanna borrow?" said Redhead.

"Five hundred," I said.

The two lugnuts traded glances like we'd made an offer to buy the Miami Heat.

"All right. The vig's ten percent a week. You'll get the odds from the bookie," said Redhead, tightening his cheek muscles in an attempt at a smile.

It was clear from the venue that we were not dealing in high-roller stakes, but I still couldn't get my head around the fact these guys were excited about a payoff that amounted to fifty bucks a week. It all seemed so small time, especially to warrant dumping a boy in the ocean. I nodded at Lucas.

"So, are they the same terms you offered our friend?" said Lucas.

"I guess," said Redhead. "Who's your friend?"

"His name is Desi," I said. "He's an eleven-year-old kid."

The two guys tightened their stance and set their jaws.

"Who the hell are you guys?"

"He said he owed you guys two hundred," said Lucas. "But he owed us some money, too. He said he had four hundred and was bringing our dough over. Thing is, he never made it."

"Got nothing to do with us," said Baldy.

"Maybe not," said Lucas, shrugging. He did everything with an economy of movement that was common in South Florida. Even his speech was relaxed.

He was the personification of what physicists called potential energy. So when he exploded into action it surprised no one more than me. In a blur of legs and fists the two big guys went to ground covered in their own blood, before I could even comprehend what was happening. It was like trying to keep my eyes on a hockey puck.

Baldy covered his nose, trying to stem the blood flow, while his hair-endowed buddy was more concerned with the kick that had sent his crown jewels into his stomach.

"You knuckleheads have no shame, taking money from a little boy." Lucas got down and took Baldy's wallet from his hip pocket. He rifled through it and counted the cash. "One forty. You better hope Blue here has the rest."

Redhead spat through gritted teeth. "Why you keep calling me Blue?"

Lucas frowned as if the question required no explanation. "Because you're a bloodnut, a redhead. Why do you think?"

Lucas grabbed Redhead's wallet and fanned it open to me. It was thick with cash—mostly tens and twenties. Lucas counted out until he reached four hundred total, then he threw the wallet on the ground.

"You maggots are dead meat, you understand?" yelled Redhead.

Lucas stood and nodded. "Old Father Time gets us all in the end."

Then he drove his boot into Redhead's face, diverting his attention. Lucas turned to Baldy, who whimpered and coiled up in the fetal position.

"How's the hangover?" said Lucas.

Baldy moaned a response.

"Yeah, I know," said Lucas, ramming his heel into Baldy's ribs with a crack. Lucas nodded his head to me, suggesting it was time to go, which I couldn't have agreed with more. We strode away from the sounds of Baldy launching his breakfast onto the gravel, and headed for my SUV.

We got back to my house on Singer Island feeling good. Perhaps those goons would think twice or even three times before hurting a kid again. I opened the front door and glanced at the sofa. The blanket was at one end, the pillow at the other. The ham sandwich had disappeared from the plate, as had the water in the now empty glass. I looked around the living room, then turned to the sound of the patio door sliding open. Danielle came inside, her face contorted with concern.

"Where's Desi?" she said.

"He's not here?" I asked.

She shook her head.

"He's gone."

CHAPTER THREE

I hadn't planned on visiting West Palm Jai Alai ever again, let alone within the hour. To say Danielle wasn't happy about us leaving Desi alone was an understatement. She was in no way placated by me telling her we had gotten his money back, any more than she was by Lucas pulling the cash from his pocket and showing it to her. She called us irresponsible and foolish, which I thought was a touch harsh, and demanded we go and find him.

"How?" I said.

"You're a PI, you'll figure it out," she said, storming out the door. "I'm going to do a sweep of the island."

We left her to do that and headed back from whence we had come. The parking lot was no more full, but the gravel behind the building was empty, save a dark patch of dried blood. We walked back in through the casino and into the jai alai court. There were four players on court now, and it appeared they were playing doubles. The other players waited on a bench near the end of the court. One of the players we had seen earlier—number twenty-five—glanced in our direction and made eye contact. He stared at me for a time, until I drew my eyes away and looked around the room.

We decided on the soft approach; splitting up and making our way through the rows, asking each man if they knew Desi or had seen the boy. There were not many men watching, and it didn't take long to reconvene on the opposite side of the seating area.

"Nothing," said Lucas.

"No one saw anything, ever," I replied.

We watched the jai alai match conclude anticlimactically with a ball that dribbled away. With much greater volume than was necessary, the announcer called the winners, and their names were displayed on the board. It seemed the day's games were over as the crowd—such as it was—shuffled out of the auditorium. The players gathered their equipment and milled about, except number twenty-five. He seemed to be keeping his eyes on us. He turned and chatted to some of his colleagues, who nodded and walked away, I guessed toward the locker room. Number twenty-five collected his things and headed our way.

Lucas and I watched him walk over as a janitor wandered into the bright lights of the court with a mop. Twenty-five had dark features and his sweat-soaked red shirt reaffirmed my thought that he looked like a polo player who had lost his mount. As he reached us I noted that the muscles on his right arm looked much stronger than his left, giving his body an asymmetrical look.

"I know you," he said to me, with a Cuban accent.

"I don't recall," I said.

"No," he shook his head. "We have never met. But I know you. I saw you play baseball. You are *the* Miami Jones."

It always caught me by surprise when people remembered me from my playing days. It had been a good few years since I had hung up the cleats, and even at my peak I'd never made it onto a card in a pack of gum.

"That so? In Port St Lucie?"

"No, you played for the Mets at Roger Dean Stadium. Against the Cardinals. You pitch good. But you lost."

"Yeah, Palm Beach had a good team that year. They won the league. Mister, that was almost ten years ago. You have a darn good memory."

"*Si*, I remember. We sit on the away-team side, and you signed a ball for my son."

I nodded. I remembered as a player, training, playing, coming off the field exhausted, getting ready for a shower and a bus ride or flight somewhere, often thinking that the last thing I wanted to do was sign autographs. But I always did, even after a loss, because somewhere in the back of my brain I remembered the ball that I had been given, at the one solitary baseball game my father had taken me to. I couldn't remember the player, and I no longer had the ball, but I never shook the special feeling that I'd had when a real-life baseball player handed me the signed ball, winked and ruffled my hair with his sweaty, clay-stained hand.

I stuck my hand out. "Miami Jones."

He shook my hand with an open smile. "Diego Alvarez. They call me Julio."

That didn't make a lot of sense to me, but I had some experience with being called something that wasn't the name my mama gave me, so I went with it.

"Okay. Nice to meet you, Julio. This is Lucas."

The two men exchanged handshakes and Julio returned his gaze to me.

"What brings you to the jai alai, Señor Miami?"

"We're looking for a boy. A Cuban boy; goes by the name of Desi."

Julio nodded and thought for a moment. "I am not sure."

"He was placing bets with the two Irish-looking *hombres* who sit up in the back."

"Those are not good men, señor."

"No, they are not. And now an eleven-year-old boy is missing."

"Such a small boy, I thought you meant older," said Julio. "This smaller boy, yes, I think I have seen him."

"Tell me."

"I do not know this boy. He is not in my community. Perhaps he is a recent arrival."

"Recent arrival? He spoke English pretty well."

"Si, sometimes the children know some English, that is why they come first. On the boats from Havana. They are small and take up less room, so they can fit more on each boat, you see?"

"Yes, I see." I had heard about the boats from Cuba. Hell, I'd seen them on TV, crossing over to Miami, looking for asylum. Even after the US had re-established political ties with Havana, the tide hadn't stemmed. In some areas it was worse. As often as not the boats, which were closer to thatched rafts, didn't make it. Those who got to US soil usually got to stay.

"I thought most Cuban refugees stayed in Miami?" I said.

"Si, they do. But we have been in Florida many years, and we have spread out. If the boy perhaps has some family here in West Palm, he may have been taken in."

"You don't have any idea where?" Lucas asked.

Julio shrugged. "As I say, he is not in my community. But sometimes the new arrivals, they have not so much money. We try to help them, through the church. Some of them live in the trailer park. *Los Piños.* Out near the turnpike. You know it?"

I nodded. "Yes, Julio, I think I do." I looked at Lucas and he nodded at me, then I turned back to Julio. "Thank you, Julio, you have been a great help."

"You are welcome, señor. I hope the boy is all right. And now I have a question of you."

"Sure, what is it?"

"You are private investigator now, correct?"

"Yes, that's right."

Julio nodded and frowned. "I have need of a private investigator."

"What do you need a private investigator for, Julio?"

"Señor, someone is trying to kill me."

CHAPTER FOUR

Julio told us that his little problem of someone wanting him dead also concerned the rest of his jai alai buddies, so we agreed to meet the group after the players had showered and changed. Lucas and I used the interval to check out his tip about Desi's location.

Los Piños, or the *The Pines*, was the kind of trailer park that gave trailer parks their bad reputation. Stuck out near the turnpike off Southern Boulevard, the grounds were a patchwork of mismatched grasses, not so much in need of mowing as napalm, and not a pine tree in sight. I had always hypothesized that if gardeners were to go on strike in South Florida it would only take a few weeks for the greenery to take over again, and Los Piños was exhibit A in support of my case. Even after the drab casino, Los Piños was a depressing place to be.

The trailers were exclusively single-wide and almost all in need of repair. A decent hurricane was going to lift this whole place up and dump it back in Cuba, at a human cost I didn't want to consider.

Small children poked their heads out from behind rusted trailers and cracked plastic furniture as we drove slowly around the park, getting our bearings. The whole place smelled of desperation, the fruition of a lie, a tale spun by seedy men in alleyways in Havana, a tale of freedom and opportunity in the great US of A. And for those that survived the crossing and ended up in Los Piños, not so much fulfillment of a dream as more of the same. We cruised a lap of the place without a plan, then slowed near the main entry.

"What do you think, chief?" said Lucas.

"When in doubt, start where you are. The nosiest people in any trailer park live near the entrance."

Lucas nodded, and I parked, and we headed out. We didn't anticipate too many invitations for coffee and cookies. As it was, the first three doors didn't open at all. Just because these were the cheapest accommodations going around didn't mean these folks weren't out looking for work. Or doing it. The hard, unpleasant stuff that those of us lucky enough to be delivered on American soil sure didn't want to do.

The fourth door opened. Close enough to the main entrance to keep an eye on all comings and goings, but far enough away to not get woken by the traffic. An old woman in a house dress opened the door as we walked up the split concrete pathway beside her ancient trailer. This thing looked like it had been on its last legs when JFK ascended the throne, and had been mended with corrugated iron and sheets of aluminum, a patchwork quilt of metals. The woman didn't speak but eyed us with suspicion, despite our best smiles. Lucas spoke better Spanish than me, so he took the lead.

"*Señora*, we are looking for Desi. Do you know Desi?"

The woman frowned and rolled her eyes mumbling something to herself, something that sounded less than complimentary to us.

"There are eight Desis live here. Every Cubano who wants to come to America calls their boy Desi and their girl Lucy."

I thought of Desi Arnez Jr., the musician husband of Lucille Ball, from the black-and-white shows my mother so loved when I was a kid in Connecticut. I wondered if that was what the refugees expected to find here, a chance to relive Havana's glory days in the Palm Beaches.

"This Desi is a boy," said Lucas. "Eleven years old."

The woman's eyes narrowed. I couldn't imagine that two scruffy blond guys looking for a small boy was a good look to anyone, let alone a nosy old Cuban woman in a trailer park.

"He lost some money," I said, hoping I had gotten the syntax right. "We have it and want to return it to him."

The woman's face didn't relax one iota, but she grunted, *Dinero?*, and we nodded, at which she put her palm up, instructing us to stay put, then she slammed the door of her trailer shut. The whole thing rocked on its foundations and continued to wobble as the woman moved about inside. The door flung open again and the woman stepped gingerly down the concrete steps. She had removed the housedress—like a full body apron— leaving her regular dress, a floral print the color of the Caribbean Sea. She waved her hand like a tour guide and we followed her along two streets, then down one. We got to a peach-colored trailer with a throng of bicycles chained up under a tarp shade, and she signaled for us to wait on the sidewalk. The woman then went to the door, knocked, and spoke to a man in a white tank top. The man listened, looked at us, then frowned, listened more, then frowned deeper. The old woman stepped back and the man came down from his trailer and grabbed a shirt that hung on one of the bicycles. It looked like a bowling shirt from another age, black with white diamonds. The man buttoned it as he walked toward us. I noticed a series of other heads pop out from the door of the trailer, checking out the *yumas*.

"Can I help you?" the man said in accented English.

"Yes, sir," I said. "We are looking for a boy called Desi. He lost some money and we wanted to make sure he got it back."

"You want to give Desi money?"

"Yes. It's his money. We sort of found it, and we wanted to return it."

"Who are you?" said the man. He didn't appear to be buying our story at all. *Come look everyone, yumas with free money!*

"My name is Miami Jones, sir. This is Lucas."

"What did you do to Desi?"

"Do? Nothing. We just have his money. We can give it to him and leave."

The man gave the beginnings of what I figured was a pretty good snarl as he looked between Lucas and me, sizing us up. "You should go," he finally said.

"But, sir—"

"Go." He didn't raise his voice, but he was firm, and we didn't want to cause these folks any trouble. Then Lucas broke into Spanish.

"*Some bad men took Desi and threw him in the ocean for his money. I jumped in and saved him. We just want to make sure he is okay.*"

"Which men?" asked the man in English.

"Bad men." Lucas looked at me, then back to the man. "We took care of them."

The man nodded as he considered this. Then his face relaxed.

"Please," he said. "Come inside."

The inside of the trailer didn't match the exterior. It was spotlessly clean and the old furniture, limited as it was, well cared for. Faux-wood paneled walls had been recently dusted, as had a picture of Jesus on the crucifix, and a small kitchen had none of the detritus of cooking that was a regular feature at my place. The man offered us a seat on an old sofa that was covered in a floral print bed sheet, similar to the old woman's dress, just red. We sat and the man took a wooden chair opposite us.

"*Agua? Cerveza?*" he said.

"*No, gracias,*" we both replied.

The man introduced himself as Miguel, and we introduced ourselves to him.

"So, Desi," he said. "I knew he had found trouble. He was away all last night, then he missed school today. The school calls Mrs. Lopez—she has a cell phone."

"Is he home?" said Lucas.

"Si. He has not spoken since he returned. He was very tired and my wife is very worried. You say he was with bad men."

I nodded.

"Where is Desi's father?" I asked.

"Desi's father is my wife's brother. He is in Cuba."

"How did Desi get here alone?"

"On the boats. It is very risky, you understand? Many people are lost. But we want to be in the United States."

"Why? Hasn't the US stopped sanctions and opened up relations with Cuba again?" I asked.

"In theory, Sénor. But there is no much work in Cuba. Children are educated, but then cannot find jobs. There is no opportunity for a nice life, you see?"

We nodded in unison.

"So we risk everything to come here. My wife's brother sends his boy because he is young and small and speaks some English. But he can only afford to send one child. The boat owners, they charge very much. Passage is expensive."

"Doesn't the United States offer emigration now?" I said.

Miguel shrugged. "It is very difficult. And more expensive. They require fees, and money in the bank, and a sponsor in the US. Many people cannot meet the criteria. And the Cuban government will not always give the visa to leave. So people still look for other ways. We know that if you get to the US, you can stay. After one year, you can become a *residente*."

"How did you get here, Miguel?" said Lucas.

"This way. But I was lucky, had some money. I could pay for me, my wife, two children. But that took all our money. We start from nothing. I find work on construction, and we come to West Palm."

"When was this?"

"Four years ago. Soon I hope we can save to move into an apartment."

I nodded and leaned forward on my thighs. "Was Desi trying to earn money to pay for his family to come over?"

Miguel nodded. "I know he collected cans, bottles, these things, for recycling. He went to the beach, to the picnics, to festivals. He worked hard. But it takes up to five thousand American dollars to pay for one passage."

"Five thousand bucks?" said Lucas.

"Si. If you want to get to land. For five hundred, smugglers will drop you off the Cuba coast, in international water, with only a tire tube. Most people who do this do not make it."

We were all silent for a moment, processing the image of people floating in the Florida Straits, grasping inner tubes, still eighty-odd miles from the United States.

"Miguel, we think that Desi tried to make some more money by betting on jai alai," I said.

Miguel's face dropped, and he rubbed his hands through his thick, dark hair. "He lose?"

"Yes, he lost."

"And these bad men, they want their money."

"Yes. But they didn't just take the money he owed. They took it all. Then to cover their tracks . . ." I looked up at Miguel's wife, standing behind her husband, concern written across her face. "To cover their tracks, they threw him in the ocean."

Miguel's wife gasped, and Miguel looked to the ceiling with a set jaw. Then he looked me in the eye. "And you saved him."

"Lucas here, he was . . . well . . . Fishing, and he saw it. He pulled Desi from the water and brought him to my house. My girlfriend, she is a sheriff. She looked after him. Then we asked him what happened, and Lucas and I went and got his money back. But when we got back to my house, Desi was gone."

Miguel's eyes darted between Lucas and me, and I saw tears gather in the corners. "And the bad men?"

"Don't worry about them," said Lucas.

"But I must," said Miguel.

"Why?" I asked.

Miguel shook his head. "Because there are many such men. There is one young man who comes here. We tell the kids to stay away, but you know kids. He's into drugs, and all sorts of bad things. Gambling, too. He doesn't live in the park, but he is here a lot. He knows there are many desperate people here."

"Who is this guy?" I said.

"He goes by the name *El Tiburon*."

"The Shark?" said Lucas.

Miguel nodded, then turned and spoke to his wife in rapid fire Spanish. She whispered to a young girl, who dashed out of the trailer.

"We owe you our lives," said Miguel.

"No," I said. "We just want to make sure the boy is all right."

The door flew open and the girl stepped back inside, followed by Desi, pushed in through the door by the nosy woman who had brought us. She retreated back out the door, and Desi stood before us, eyes glued to the floor. He was small for his age, and he seemed to have shrunk a couple inches from his ordeal.

"Hi Desi," I said.

The boy didn't respond, which was pretty much status quo for our relationship.

"Mr. Lucas is here. He has your money. He got it back."

"G'day, Desi," said Lucas, standing and moving to the boy. He pulled the wad of cash from his pocket and crouched over, hands on knees, to look Desi in the eye. "Here's your money, Desi."

Desi looked up a little, at the money.

"Now I am going to give this back to you, okay?" said Lucas. "Your uncle will hold it for you. As long as you promise me you won't go near those bad men again."

The color washed from Desi's face, looking as it did when he'd first arrived at my door in Lucas's arms.

"What is this money for?" said Lucas.

Desi lifted his head and looked at Lucas. "Papa."

"Right. So let's not waste it. Okay?"

Desi nodded gently, then retreated into the arms of his aunt.

Lucas handed the cash to Miguel.

"You'll see it's kept safe and used to get the boy's family back?" Lucas had an easy manner about him, but in that one sentence it evaporated. There was subtext dripping from the words, and we all got his meaning. *Don't you be keeping it for yourself, uncle.*

"Si. Some of his earnings must go to our living expenses, you understand. He is another mouth to feed. But most will be kept to get my wife's brother and his family here. We all save as much as we can for this."

Lucas nodded.

"How long will it take to save enough to bring the family over?" I said.

Miguel shook his head slowly. "Many years, señor. For the whole family, many years."

"They can't send another child?"

Miguel shook his head, with more vigor. "No. Desi has two sisters. We do not send the girls alone. Many bad things can happen to girls between there and here."

I got his meaning. I couldn't imagine the desperation a father must feel to put his only son on a woven raft with smugglers and set him out to sea.

Lucas and I made our farewells, and Miguel thanked us and showed us out. As we stepped through the door, Miguel's wife gave each of us a kiss on the cheek. Reward enough, that's for sure. Desi hovered behind his aunt but offered Lucas a tight little smile. Lucas beamed and ruffled the boy's hair.

We wandered back to our car in the cool evening air, content that our good deed was done. But as I slipped into my SUV, I couldn't shake an uncomfortable feeling. Lucas strapped in and turned to me.

"Those mongrels are just gonna do that to another kid. You know that, right?"

And there it was. Thank you, Dr. Lucas. "I do."

"I think it's time you earned your biscuits, Mr. Private Eye. Find out who those goons work for."

"Yeah, I can do that."

"I gotta get back to Miami," he said as I pulled out of the trailer park. "I left the kid in charge of the marina today, but two days in a row is way risky."

"I'll do some digging," I said. "I find something, I'll call."

"Do that."

I pulled out of the trailer park and headed back to drop Lucas at his truck. I watched him as I drove. He seemed relaxed, like he'd spent the day at the beach. He didn't waste any energy. Once a thing was done, it was done, then it was time to wait for the next thing. As I headed back to Singer Island I formulated a plan to track down this El Tiburon, and I tried to keep my own energy in reserve, so it was all saved up and ready to go when I found him.

CHAPTER FIVE

Havana wasn't the most imaginative name for a restaurant, but it was accurate. Stepping through the potted palms surrounding the door was like stepping into Cuba circa 1950. There were black-and-white pictures of musicians and classic cars and all that Buena Vista Social Club stuff. It looked like a hell of a time, like Palm Springs with Sinatra. The tables in the place were dark wood and the drapes red velvet. A waiter in a white shirt and black bow tie gave me a welcoming smile.

"Julio," I said, by way of explanation.

The waiter nodded like I'd dropped the secret password and led me through the back of the dining room, past the bathrooms, and out into a small courtyard. Plush sofas and rattan armchairs sat under white canvas drapes, and soft jazz seemed to emanate from the palms that surrounded the whole area. There were twelve men in the courtyard, all dressed in shirt-sleeves and trousers.

Most had their sleeves rolled up, and some were partaking of cigars. They all shared a common dark feature set, like their lineage hit a common point in Spain around the time of the conquistadors. It was a classy-looking group, and I was glad it was winter and I had chosen khakis over shorts. One of the men turned to me, and I saw it was Julio. He looked like he had at the fronton, clean-cut and athletic, of slim build and strong right side. I glanced around the courtyard and noticed that the other men shared the look.

Julio smiled. "Señor Miami." He swapped his beer into his left hand and shook mine.

"It's just Miami, Julio."

"Of course, señor. Would you care for cerveza?" he said.

"Sure," I said. This was my kind of crowd.

Julio gave the waiter a nod and he did a half bow and trotted away. "Come, meet the *pelotari*."

"The what?"

"The pelotari," he said, waving his hand theatrically across the group of men, who all responded with smiles and nods.

"This is what we call the players of jai alai, the pelotari."

I nodded as the waiter returned with my beer, complete with lime wedge. I'm not one for fruit with my beer, but when in Rome . . . I held my drink up to the group and they returned the gesture.

"This is Roto," said Julio, pointing to a guy in an armchair, who stood and shook my hand.

"And this is Domingo. This here is Perez, and this is Benicio."

Julio made the rounds of the entire group, introducing each by the one name.

"It's like the Brazilian football team," I smiled.

Julio frowned.

"Everyone has just one name."

"Si," he nodded. "This also is jai alai tradition. The game is originally from the Basque region of *Espana*, Spain, and it is tradition when a pelotari begins his career, he chooses a single name by which he is known for the rest of his life. Some, it is their family name, some their hometown. Others simply choose a name, like as you say, a famous football player or musician."

Julio offered me a rattan chair and sat himself.

"So Julio, you mentioned that you were in danger, that someone wanted to harm you?"

"Si, someone has made threats," he said.

The man called Roto said something in Spanish, too rapidly for me to pick anything up.

"With your permission, Roto will translate into Spanish for the rest of the men," said Julio. "Most of us speak English okay, but some not so much. And we are all brothers in this together."

"Sure, that's fine."

Roto did his thing, and Julio kept going.

"It began recently. I received a note in my locker in the fronton. Some of the others did also. The notes said to stop promoting the jai alai—to leave it be."

"Promoting it?"

"Si, I should go back. Jai alai is a dying game, Señor Miami. When I was a boy, jai alai was the biggest game in town. The fronton was a popular destination. Many thousands of people came to see the performances."

"Performances?"

"Si, this is what we call the session of games; a performance. In the seventies and early eighties the jai alai was a social scene. In Miami fronton, over fifteen thousand people would watch, up here in West Palm as many as ten thousand. Everyone dressed up, suits and dresses. The box at the back of our fronton held corporate suites and a dining room. It was the most popular game in South Florida."

Roto translated, and the group all nodded as one.

"So what happened?" I said.

"Many things, señor. Back at this time, South Florida had no NBA team, no baseball. Outside of the Miami Dolphins football, jai alai was the main professional sport. Then the NBA came—the Heat—and the ice hockey and the Marlins baseball. And at the same time, jai alai did not promote so well. There was a player strike, and the crowds went away. Now you see what it has become. We play for maybe fifty people on a good night, a Saturday evening performance. There is no dress code, and most people just come for the betting."

I nodded and sipped my beer, as did everyone else. Then Julio continued.

"We see the future, Señor Miami. It is not so good for the professional pelotari. The game dies. The casino is more interested in promoting card games and the seafood buffet. So we take things into our own hands. We collect together to promote jai alai. I am elected by my colleagues to create a plan, to promote our game in the area. To bring more people to the performances, to recruit more players. Maybe the great days are gone, but we do not believe that our game should die."

"I understand," I said, and I did. Old traditions die hard. But I also knew that, more often than not, die they eventually did. Croquet was pretty big once, or so I hear. Polo too. Thing was, polo was still a niche product, and attracted a pretty wealthy crowd. I supposed that jai alai could keep on, with a bit of work, and these men didn't look shy of work.

"Okay, Julio. Tell me what happened, with the threats."

"Yes, the threats. Letters in our lockers, they tell us to stop promoting the game. You see, our efforts were working. One weekend we have ten people in the audience, then the next week we have twenty, then fifty. We get on the local news and attract over one hundred people to a matinee. Then the notes say to stop it."

"And did you?"

Several of the group snorted, as if it were a preposterous thought.

"No," said Julio. "We kept on with our efforts."

"And what happened?"

"Last week, I received a message. Written in, how do you say it? The water from your breath?" Julio huffed into his palm to illustrate.

"Condensation?"

"Si, condensation. The letters were written in the condensation on the window of my car."

"How do you know it wasn't just a prank—someone walking by?"

"No señor, you misunderstand. The writing, the condensation was on the inside of the car. And the car was locked."

That changed things some. "And what did the message say this time?"

"Stop jai alai or die."

"Well at least it's poetic."

"Señor?"

"Nothing."

Julio looked to his colleagues and got a group nod. "So señor, you will take the case?"

Each of the men started standing or wriggling in their seats, pulling cash out of their wallets or pockets. They began passing wads of cash to Julio.

"We can pay," said Julio.

I put my palms up. "Whoa boys, hold on. I can see you're good for it. Just hold your money. I'll take the case. I'll look into it for you."

Julio smiled and Roto translated, then the rest of the men smiled. They held their cash toward me.

"Roto, tell them I'll invoice you, okay?" I turned to Julio. "So who do you think is behind it. Who wants your jai alai promotion to fail so badly?"

"We don't know, señor. We think maybe there is another casino who wants us out of business."

"Another fronton?"

Julio shook his head. "I think not, Señor Miami. We have many friends at other frontons, and we often play each other. Our success would be their success."

"So who, then?" I said.

"Well, I don't like to say it."

"This is just between you and me, Julio."

"The big casinos. The Indians."

CHAPTER SIX

When I got back from meeting the pelotari, I was tired and needed to switch off for a while. It was one of those times I wished I had a television. I opened the door and found Danielle sitting at the kitchen counter. She was in plain clothes; jeans and a T-shirt. I always looked forward to walking in the front door and seeing her smile. It was one of those smiles, a real traffic stopper. But there was no traffic hitting the brakes tonight. There was no smile. She spun on her stool with a frown.

"Did you find him?"

"Yes," I smiled, hero of the hour.

"Why didn't you call me?"

"What? I just found him, like an hour ago."

"An hour? You don't have a cell phone? I've been sitting here, worried."

I threw my keys in the bowl and put my hand on her shoulder. "I'm sorry, sweetheart. I didn't think a few minutes was going to make a difference."

She pushed my hand away and stood. "You're such an idiot. You don't think a few minutes make a difference? You don't think. How about this morning? Were you thinking when you left a small boy alone?"

"He's not that small, he's eleven. Besides, we went to find who threw him in the ocean. I didn't know he'd run away."

She shook her head as she walked away. "I've been at work since 3 a.m. I'm going to bed."

I watched Danielle stride into the bedroom and close the door, my jaw open to somewhere around my navel. I waited for a moment to gather my thoughts. Sure, I didn't feel great that Desi had run away, but he wasn't under house arrest, and we were trying to find the guys who had attempted to murder him. It wasn't like we'd ducked out to Longboard's for a couple beers. And we'd spent the rest of the day hunting him down, which we had succeeded in doing. So no autopsy, no foul.

I cracked the door open and stepped into the dark bedroom. I could hear Danielle breathing—rapid not relaxed—a long way from sleep. I sat on the bed and put my hand on her arm.

"I'm sorry," I said, although I wasn't completely sure what I was apologizing for. "I should have taken more care, but we found him. He's okay. And we got his money back."

Danielle let out a big sigh. "I'm just really tired. Let's talk in the morning."

I kissed her cheek and left her to sleep, returning to the kitchen. I was hungry but my hunger was only matched by my apathy. I couldn't be bothered opening a pickle jar, let alone making dinner. Instead, I poured a scotch and wandered out onto the patio. The night was cool, and as I sat on my lounger I wondered what had happened to the sweatshirt I had put on Desi. But Florida in winter is no great hardship, so I sat in shirtsleeves and warmed myself from the inside, with hints of tobacco and peat. Watching the water was where I did my best thinking. It was why I had bought the house—the only original rancher left, right on the Intracoastal side of the island. After I picked it up for a song at a tax lien auction, I had surprised all the other residents by doing absolutely no renovations whatsoever. It was a seventies original, just like me, and just like me, it was aging naturally and with a distinct lack of grace. But this evening the water and tinkling of masts didn't weave their magic. My brain wouldn't relax, and I felt the energy bubbling inside of me. I couldn't shake the bad feeling inside, as if the thing with the bad guys who had hurt Desi was going to get bad before it got good, and that maybe the same could be said for things with Danielle. The look on her face was as if the Desi thing had revealed something in my character, something she hadn't seen before, something she really didn't like. It wasn't the first time I had messed up, and it wasn't the first time I had cleaned up my own mess. But

her look said something had changed. I sipped my Scotch
to drown that thought, and eventually fell asleep.

I must have woken at some point in the night,
because when the morning light hit I was in bed. I rolled
over to put a hand on Danielle but came up with nothing
but sheet. I padded out into the kitchen to make a
smoothie. Winter in Florida is a good time for kale, and
the best way to eat kale is in a smoothie. It really does
taste rotten, but everyone assured me it was the healthiest
food on the entire planet, so I blended it up with some
peeled Florida oranges and some hempseed. I was just
pouring when Danielle came bursting through the sliding
door, breathing heavily and covered in a sheen of
perspiration. Her hair was tied back, and her running tank
top and tight shorts left just the right amount to the
imagination.

"Hey," she said.

"Hey," I replied, the epitome of linguistic
sophistication.

"You went for a run?" I said.

"Yeah."

"You didn't wake me."

"I thought you'd want the sleep."

She'd never left me to sleep in lieu of a run before,
short of having busted ribs, and I hadn't hit the beach for
a jog in ages, despite it having been a daily habit not so
long ago.

"Okay. You want some smoothie?"

"Sure, thanks. I'm just going to jump in the shower."

I delivered the smoothie to the steam-filled bathroom and considered getting in with her, but the internal radar said go easy, and although I didn't understand the source of the signal, I still knew what a flashing red light meant. When Danielle came out, she was in uniform and drying her hair with a towel. She dropped the finished glass in the sink.

"Thanks for the smoothie."

"Sure, anytime. Kitchen's always open."

Danielle kept rubbing at her hair as she wandered back into the bedroom. When she came out again she was buttoned up, her dry hair tied back. She came over to the counter where I was washing out the blender.

"Listen, MJ, I'm sorry about last night. I was just tired, is all. And worried about Desi."

The worry had been plain for all to see. It was the rest of the look that concerned me, but I didn't have a clue how to verbalize it, so I left it alone until I could figure it out.

"It's okay. I get it. I was pretty worried myself. I just don't deal with kids all that much, you know? It didn't occur that he'd run off. But lesson learned."

"Yeah. And he's okay?"

"Sheepish, but fine. He's got some family here, so they'll look after him."

"I didn't find much out yesterday, but I did hear from a friend at the ER."

"That right?"

"Aha. She said they had a couple known crime figures, low-grade thugs, come into the hospital, beat up pretty bad."

"I suppose it's an occupational hazard."

"Doesn't usually happen at lunchtime."

I made a face that resembled a guppy, and Danielle came around and laid a kiss on me. "I have to get to work," she said. "You got a good day planned?"

"Peachy. I'm gonna go see your ex-husband."

Danielle shook her head as she grabbed her keys.

"Play nice."

CHAPTER SEVEN

Eric Edwards, state attorney for the fifteenth Judicial Circuit, was a man with a plan. I couldn't fathom why else he would be guest of honor at the opening of a new therapy pool at a senior citizens center in Palm Beach. Sure, state attorneys were elected, but this was above and beyond. This smelled of higher ambitions. He was a smooth operator, I had to give him that. He looked sharp in his tailored suit and silk tie, the double-breasted jacket padding out his stick-figure frame to regular man size. He spoke well and charmed the diapers off the old girls in the center. I stood at the back of the room while he had coffee and cake, and noted that despite being handed several plates, none of the cake actually passed his lips.

He bounded out of the center in full confab mode with his assistant, a petite, blond, pocket rocket called Anastasia. Eric certainly had a type, and it hadn't changed despite an affair that led to the collapse of his marriage to

Danielle. The fact she ended up with a scruffy piece of work like me must have rubbed him the wrong way in a major fashion, but seeing me didn't break Eric's stride.

"Well if it isn't Magnum, P.I. You're on the wrong island, aren't you, Jones?"

"Not at all, Eric. These are my people."

"I doubt that. Your right-hand man might be dating one of Palm Beach's society ladies, but that isn't you."

It was true; it wasn't me. My right-hand man, Ron, had met Cassandra, a well-heeled widow on the island, during a previous case, and they had become a bit of an item. But Eric didn't care. He strode by me toward his car.

"Palm Beach society lady? I'd call Lady Cassandra more a donor-in-waiting."

Eric stopped dead and turned to me. "Waiting for what?"

"The right candidate to support," I smiled.

Eric ran his hand down his tie, smoothing it out, like his fingers were little steam presses.

"What do you want, Jones?"

"I thought to myself this morning, you know, I haven't had lunch with old Eric in a while."

"You're a card, Jones."

"That's what they tell me. No, I just know that the incumbent local member of the Florida Legislature is a big supporter of the Seminole tribe, and there might be benefit in your knowing that they may be up to no good."

Eric's assistant drove us to The Breakers, and Eric, as a local celeb of sorts, was able to get us a table in the seafood bar. The Breakers was a palatial resort on the beach, an institution on the island. It was full of old, expensive things for a mostly old, expensive clientele. Although I had more of a McDonald's budget, I figured Eric was good for the intel.

"The Seminole are a hot potato," he said, sipping his ice water.

"Interesting metaphor. But they are also happy to back every horse in the race just to ensure they're on the winner."

"As SA, I can't get support from them if they are up to any criminal activity."

"So let me make sure they're not. And if they are, you have something on your opponent."

"I don't have an opponent, Jones. I'm not running for anything."

"Of course not. So what can you tell me about the Seminole?"

"What do you want to know?" said Eric.

A platter of stone crab arrived at our table, and as the server left I continued. "Help me understand the Compact," I said.

Eric cracked open a claw but didn't go for the mustard sauce. "The Compact is an agreement, a contract between the Seminole Nation and the state of Florida, that gives the tribe exclusive rights to certain card games and all slots in the state, outside of Broward and Miami-Dade counties."

"I thought the casinos were on tribal land. How does the state have any say?"

"They don't have a say over the casinos. The tribe is considered a sovereign nation. As a sovereign nation, they pay no federal income tax, and the state cannot tax or levy them without offering something in return."

"And that something is exclusive rights."

"Exactly," he said, going in for more crab. He sure loved to eat on someone else's dime. "And it's not a tax, it's actually a revenue-share arrangement. The state agrees there will be no competition, and in return gets a cut—currently somewhere around two hundred-plus million dollars a year."

"That's a lot of change."

"It is, which is why it's a political hot potato. Other groups want to bring destination casinos to Florida, and then there are the racinos—they'd like to grow. But if the state allows that, the Seminole are within their rights to give the State absolutely nothing. It's a balancing act. If the State allows other casinos to have slots, will they make more in tax revenue than they will lose from the Seminole revenue share? And if so, at what cost? There's a social agenda to consider here. Lots of people are against more casinos, mainly because of the negative effects of gambling."

I pulled some meat from a crab claw and sucked it down. It was sweet, and the claws themselves were beautiful to look at. I'm sure the crabs they came from would argue they looked better in situ.

"So how does jai alai fit into all this?" I said.

Eric frowned as he sipped water. "Jai alai? They're the pari-mutuels."

"Yeah, right. How does that work?"

Eric ate a bite and took a moment. He liked the spotlight, even if it was just me with a flashlight. "You have to understand that gaming legislation in Florida is piecemeal," he said. "Things were just made up on the fly as they came up, with no real strategy in place. That makes some of these laws look strange now. Pari-mutuels are like that. They are essentially sports establishments that have been given limited gambling rights to supplement the sport. I'm talking jai alai, horse racing, and greyhounds. The latter two are known as racinos, combination racing and casino."

Eric took a sip of water and continued. "Jai Alai was essentially introduced to the US for betting, and this was way back when it was as big as football in South Florida. In Broward and Miami-Dade some of these places have slots and cards, others just cards. But the law says the pari-mutuels have to keep their racing or jai alai to keep their gaming license, even though the sports stuff now loses money and the casino operations subsidize them."

The server came and took our platter and offered us desert, which we declined in favor of coffee.

"So why keep that law? Why not just allow them to gamble and drop the racing or jai alai?"

"Tallahassee works in mysterious ways," he said. It was true; they did. The politicians in the Florida state capital were like politicians everywhere; they could be guaranteed to do only one thing consistently, and that was to act in their own self-interest.

"The fact is," Eric continued, "the politicians like the imagery of the racing and jai alai. It's very Florida. Plus, there are a lot of jobs associated with those activities, non-tribal, voting jobs. And then there's the Compact to consider."

"So can the Compact change?"

"Sure, theoretically. It's actually coming up for renewal."

"And will it change?"

"I don't know. I don't see it. Here's the thing, and if you repeat this I'll deny it to the point of suing you for slander," said Eric.

"Because my day isn't complete without shooting off a few quotes from the great Eric Edwards."

He gave a look that I assumed was his *I'm serious* look, which might have had his interns quivering in their undies but didn't do too much for me. "There's no incentive to change, not for the politicians," he said. "The Seminole give both sides of the legislature millions in campaign money, as do lobby groups for the Vegas interests who would love a piece of the Florida action. Even the pari-mutuels give campaign money. So the longer Tallahassee kicks that can down the road, the longer that money continues. The lobby groups involved can't afford to just stop giving."

"Explains why our federal government gets nothing done, regardless of who's in the big chair," I said.

"Don't kid yourself, that's exactly why."

Our coffee arrived, and we sipped in silence for a while.

"So I've got a client who claims someone wants to shut down the jai alai game in West Palm. Any ideas who that might be?"

Eric shrugged. "Could be anyone. The Seminoles, who want it all, but I'd have thought they'd see the pari-mutuels as chump change. Then there's Vegas. If the pari-mutuels were all to fail, those jobs and taxes would disappear, and Vegas destination casinos might claim they could pick up the slack. Then there are the other pari-mutuels. They're all losing patronage, but have to keep doing the races or jai alai and continue bearing all the costs that entails. So they might think they can get a few more folks in if there's less competition."

We finished our lunch and walked out to the lobby where Anastasia sat waiting with a tall iced tea.

"So what about my donor-in-waiting?" asked Eric.

"Lady Cassandra? I'll have a word with Ron, make an introduction."

"Good. You can get back to your car, right?"

Eric's generosity had reached its bounds, but I was okay with that, because I didn't find his company all that engaging, nor he mine. I almost never wore a skirt. He took off with his lovely assistant, and I wandered back out onto the promenade and down onto the sand. The day was mild but sunny and the snowbirds were out in force, under umbrellas and cabanas, sipping fruity drinks. I pulled out my cell phone and called my right-hand man.

"Ron Bennett," he said.

"You don't have caller ID?"

"Miami. I didn't look. I'm walking. At my age you have to keep your eyes on the road."

"Where are you, old man?"

"Worth Avenue. Just finished with the German banker."

"The one who thinks his gardener is breaking into his secure computer system and stealing his ones and zeros?" I asked.

"That's him. Turns out his maid has a degree in computer science from Ohio State."

"You don't say."

"Yup. So I'm just finished here. You at the office?"

"The Breakers."

"And here I am with a fat check burning a hole in my pocket."

"Get over here," I said. "Let me put that fire out for you."

CHAPTER EIGHT

Ron and I had a couple of celebratory beers overlooking the water, waiting for the sun to start dropping behind us toward the gulf. Then he drove us to the oceanfront apartment of his squeeze, the Lady Cassandra. I had no idea if she was really a lady, like a duchess or a princess or something, but she sure had the class of one. And despite Ron's red cheeks and a face covered in the splotches of removed skin cancers, she had been utterly charmed by him. He had that way about him, and ladies of a certain age were often suckers for the wiles of Ron Bennett. But this time, he was as taken with her as she was with him. He still had his place in West Palm, but he was spending more and more time at the widow's palatial digs. Cassandra was off playing tennis, so we left Ron's car and walked back to the Escape. It was time to go shark hunting.

"You know, I like this car," he said, as I pulled out toward the bridge, back to the mainland.

"Yeah, it's boring but it does have a nice high ride."

"Perfect car for kids."

"If I run into any kids I'll be sure to ask them what they drive."

Ron smiled as we crossed the Intracoastal and headed out to Los Piños. It was the sublime to the ridiculous. Palm Beach was some of the most exclusive property on the planet, the sort of waterfront mansions that never even made the real estate section, but in twenty minutes we were in the soup of desperation and hope known as a low-rent trailer park.

I pulled the car into the lot of a liquor store where three hombres in bandanas looked my SUV over like hyenas spying a New York strip. We sat for a time watching the entrance to Los Piños as the sun fell behind us. I figured the darkness would suit El Tiburon better, and I was right. Just as boredom was setting in, we saw a black Corvette with the vanity plate *tiburon* cruise into the park. We got out and locked the Escape.

"There's not going to a problem with my car, is there?" I said to the bandanas.

One of them smiled wide. "Nah, man. We'd have to pay to get rid of them parts."

I nodded at them. It was true. Not even the local hoods were interested in my car, and for a moment I longed for my red Mustang convertible that had been smashed by some bad dudes who had wanted to hurt me.

And hurt me they did. They had busted me up pretty bad, with a hockey stick as I recalled, and then smashed my Mustang into a tree. In my fragile state I had replaced the totaled Mustang with the Escape, and the hurt lingered on and on. I glanced back at the Escape as Ron and I crossed the road.

"See, the benefits of a small SUV keep on coming," he said with a grin.

"Keep talking, pal. You drive a Camry."

"My point exactly. Fine car it is, too."

We didn't get twenty steps into the trailer park before the old woman in the house-dress popped out of her trailer. She pointed across a rusted up children's playground, to the trailers on the other side of the park.

"El Tiburon," she whispered.

I waved. "Gracias."

We wandered across the unkempt grass and found the Corvette parked at the end of a row of rusted trailers. No one was on the street. It felt like Dodge City, when the outlaws came to town. Some things never change.

"Which one do you think he's in?"

"No way of telling," I said, looking around. We could sit tight and wait to see if he came out, or if someone went in, but he might not even be on this street. I didn't have the patience for more stakeout. I had tried to keep my powder dry, to keep my energy in potential like Lucas would do, but I was done with that. I was about to explode. Being back in the trailer park reminded me of what these people had done to Desi—and would keep doing, if someone didn't show them the path to righteousness. I wandered over to a trailer that looked uninhabitable and saw the glow of a TV through the window. I picked up a weathered piece of two-by-four and walked back to the Corvette.

"He might have a gun," said Ron.

"Yeah, you're right. Go stand over there," I said, nodding across the street. Ron retreated to the shadows, and I swung the piece of wood like it was a Louisville Slugger. I had played most of my professional baseball career under the designated hitter rule, so I didn't get many at-bats. It gave pitchers a lot of room for bravado, to talk up their slugging ability when they never really had to face up at home plate. But it also meant there was a lot of pent-up energy, for all the grand slams that never were. I put all my home runs never taken into that piece of wood, and swung for the bleachers. The side mirror on the Corvette took flight, long and true, into the middle of the blacktop some fifty yards down the road. I gave myself a little whistle and waited, but no one came out. I wandered around the car and tried switch-hitting. This time I just connected, smashing the mirror but not moving the housing at all. My second try at it took the housing off and sprayed it into the window of a nearby trailer.

"Ah, foul ball."

I dropped the wood onto the ground and stepped back into the shadows on the opposite side of the road from Ron. The trailer next to me rocked violently and two guys charged out, bouncing off each other in their haste. A third guy ran to the car and inspected the damage.

"Are you kidding me?" he screamed. He looked up the street, then spun the other way, as if the perpetrator was dumb enough to be standing in the middle of the road.

"I am going kill whoever done this! Look at my car, man."

The other two guys hung back with their palms in the air. This told me two things. One was that the angry dude was the guy I was looking for, and two, the other two guys were probably not packing heat. El Tiburon certainly was. He snatched a big silver piece from his belt and waved it around like he was Pancho Villa.

"Find them!" he screamed. "They got to be here somewhere."

"Holy crap," I said, stepping out of the shadows.

El Tiburon spun and pointed the gun at me.

"Who the hell are you?" said El Tiburon.

"Did you see what that guy did? He smashed your car for a home run."

"Who did this? Tell me!" he yelled, waving the gun at everyone.

"That guy, he ran down there," I said, pointing along the street.

"Where?"

"There. He hit your mirrors for a home run, dude. With this thing." I bent over and picked up the two-by-four. I held it up for El Tiburon's buddies to see.

"See, he used this. Like a bat."

"Find him!" El Tiburon screamed at his guys.

"He just swung it like this," I said, and I hefted the wood for one last swing, hard and true and straight into El Tiburon's face. It wasn't subtle in any way, but I wasn't messing with a lunatic with a gun. And I had a little energy left that I needed to use up. I could have tried just talking to him, but these guys never seem like the diplomatic type. El Tiburon fell like a dead weight onto the grass, dropping the weapon. I picked it up. It was heavy, and that told me it was loaded. El Tiburon screamed. His nose had exploded as noses do, not a lot of damage but a lot of gore. Shock and awe, of a sort. I gestured for the other two guys to come stand by the Corvette, and they complied. Ron wandered over and patted them down, finding nothing, then I told them to sit on the ground, crisscross, apple sauce. I bent down to El Tiburon and pulled him against the car door.

"Hey, it's okay. It's just blood, all right. You're not dying, so stop the wailing."

"Aaaargh, you hit me. You are a dead man."

"Dead man?" I said, holding the gun up. He pulled the volume back to a whimper.

"What is your name?" I said.

"El Tibur—"

"No genius, not your stage name. Your real name."

"Brandon," he sobbed, looking at the blood on his hands.

"Brandon? Are you serious?" I shrugged. "Okay, Brandon. You've been selling drugs and organizing illegal bets in this park, correct?"

"You can't prove nothing."

It was true, but the truth was getting boring, so I smacked Brandon's forehead with the butt of the gun.

"I'm not a cop, Brandon. I'm not trying to prove anything. But these things you've been doing, they're going to stop. You don't come here anymore. You understand?"

He nodded his head, but I wasn't feeling full compliance, so I stood, grabbed the two-by-four, and put it through the driver's side window. Shards of glass rained down on Brandon.

"Do you understand?"

This time the nodding was vigorous.

"If you come back here, I will know. And next time the blood won't stop. Understand?"

More vigorous nodding.

"Okay. One last thing. You are not some criminal genius. You're running numbers for someone. I need to know who."

He shook his head.

"Brandon?" I said, like a schoolteacher.

"I don't run nothing, man. I just recruit. I just tell 'em where to go, and I get a finder's fee. That's all."

"And where do you tell them to go?"

"The fronton. They talk to some guys there, that's it."

I knew the guys. Redhead and Baldy. "What about if they are already a customer? What if those guys are not there?"

"They go to the fronton, they text me. Then I text the van."

"The van?"

"That's all I know."

"Okay," I said. I pulled Brandon away from the car and laid him down so I could grab his phone and car keys from his pocket. I held up the phone.

"I'm going to borrow this." Then I held up the keys. "These I'm taking so you don't do something stupid. I'll drop them at the front entry of the trailer park. In ten minutes you get up and you go get them. Anything before, I might just have to shoot you."

We left them on the grass, staring hard at the trailer in front of them. I dropped the keys to the Corvette at the edge of the road near the entrance, then Ron and I headed for the Escape. The car was in fine shape, and I waved the gun at the bandanas, just a friendly fellow saying hi. They waved back, which was nice.

"You know," said Ron. "For a guy who's not keen on violence, you're pretty adept at it."

"When you're in China, you got to speak Chinese. Even if it doesn't roll off the tongue so nice."

"What now?" Ron asked.

"Longboard Kelly's. I need a beer." I put the gun into the console between us. "And Mick will know what to do with this gun so no one ever finds it."

CHAPTER NINE

The next morning dawned like the one before: wonderfully sunny, but a touch cool if you were Floridian; perfect beach weather if you were from Quebec. The Atlantic coast of Florida had a population that ebbed and flowed like the tide, vast numbers of snowbirds descending from the Northeast and Canada, escaping those brutal winters I had grown up with, for the sun and sea and golf and all-you-can-eat buffets of Florida. I-75 and I-95 were like one-way streets headed south after Thanksgiving, then north in March and April. The town traffic came and went with the snowbirds, too, and we found ourselves cruising down A1A at no more than ten miles per hour, plenty of time to take in the rows of strip malls and gas stations.

It was time to get back on the case I was being paid for and check out what was going on with the pelotari's employers. I had left home without breakfast, Danielle having come and gone in the night, one shift to another, the sheriff's office busier during the season, just like everyone else. I dropped by my office to collect Ron, who sat on the steps of our building in the shadow of the massive courthouse complex. Our building was newer than anything around it and suited the other tenants— lawyers, bankers, some companies with those names made up by joining two unrelated words or the names of your kids—better than us. Ron stood as I pulled up, brandishing a couple coffees and a bag of bacon and egg bagels. At our breakneck speed through West Palm, we had plenty of time to eat.

We were rubbing our hands with napkins as I pulled into the near-empty parking lot at the Jai Alai and Casino. Ron and I wandered into the front entrance, once more startled by the lack of slot machine noise. Card games were pretty quiet if you thought about it, even more so when there was only one table open and no one playing at it. The few cars in the lot had brought their owners for the buffet breakfast.

"I'm gonna take a look around," said Ron.

"I'll find you after," I said, slipping between tables, toward a hallway that was marked *administration*. The hall was guarded by a big unit with an unruly haircut, the kind of scruffiness one never saw in a Vegas casino—at least not on the strip.

"I'm here to see Mr. Almondson," I said.

"You got an appointment?" said the big unit, sweating with the effort.

"Yeah."

The guy blinked hard at me, then nodded as much as a human with no discernible neck can. "Okay. There's the elevator."

I wandered past and hit the button for the elevator, then turned to look at the guy. He was facing the casino floor, empty as it was, not worried about me at all, which told me plenty. I left the elevator to do its business and hit the fire stairs. This wasn't the Empire State Building. I was pretty certain I could make it to the second floor under my own steam. I did just that and found myself in a small reception lobby. There was a desk with a box on it, and a note to hit the button in the middle of the box to call someone. I did that, then looked around. The room did not fit my idea of a casino HQ. It looked like a thousand small business offices—lawyers or tech start-ups or film production companies, any business that was on its way but had not yet cashed up enough to find nicer custom digs. The furniture was well tended but well used, and the artwork consisted of shots of people holding poker hands, mouths open, amazed that they were winning.

A small woman with a tight bun came out from one of the offices and gave me the Florida smile. It's true we get our fair share of grumpy folks, especially in season, when the snowbirds bring their moans and groans with them. But most people who come to Florida, and those who choose to stay, do so because they like it. They like swimming in winter, they like grilling year-round and they like pleasant evenings on the lanai of their two-bedroom efficiency unit with golf course glimpses. This small woman was no different. Her smile told me she had grown up somewhere cold, and even on its worst day, this was a whole lot better.

"Can I help you, sir?"

"Good morning," I smiled. "My name is Miami Jones. I'm an investigator representing employees of the casino in a workplace complaint. I was hoping for a moment of Mr. Almondson's time."

The skin between the woman's eyebrows pinched some, and she nodded. "Let me check for you."

She stepped back into her office and I waited. Without an appointment, I found the possibility of workplace revolt opened a lot of business doors. The woman reappeared and smiled again, this time a little less genuine. She ushered me in the door and led me to the end of the hall, to the big office in the corner. She knocked and we went in.

The office was massive but sparely furnished. A desk with one chair on either side, a smaller round coffee table with two arm-chairs, and nothing else. The pictures on the wall were all of building exteriors, casino projects, lit up like Christmas. The wall behind the desk was floor-to-ceiling glass and overlooked the rear of the parking lot and the freeway. The man who came out from behind the desk was surprising in a couple of ways. Everything I had seen in the casino wore the stench of being well past its prime—downmarket, you might say. But this person was anything but downmarket. Sharp pinstripe suit that fit like a glove, clearly bespoke and tailored by someone who knew what they were doing. The second surprising thing was that the man wasn't a man at all.

"I am Jenny Almondson," she said, extending her hand with a tight smile. As we shook, I got a good dose of a fruity scent. She smelled as good as she looked.

"Miami Jones," I said.

"You're here about some kind of workplace issue?"

"Of a fashion."

"Please," she said, directing me to the solitary visitor's chair by her desk.

"Would you care for coffee?" she said, striding around the desk to her own chair.

"Ice water?" I said, and she nodded to the woman with the bun, who bowed her head and left the room.

"Who is it you represent?" she asked.

I looked her over. She had shoulder-length blond hair, well groomed, that fell across one ear. In the other ear I saw a gold earring, two strands that wrapped around each other, like a model of DNA. She wore little makeup, but what was there was effective. I guessed her to be around forty, but with women's ages I always gave myself a margin of error of plus or minus twenty years. All in all, she was a very beautiful woman.

"Are you all right?" she asked, when I failed to respond to her question or take my eyes off her.

"You're a woman."

She smiled. "You're very observant."

"The casino website just refers to you J. Almondson, no photo."

"Does it make me less capable of assisting you, that I'm a woman?"

"Not at all," I said. "I guess I just had a preconception about what a casino manager would be."

"Yes, I love those preconceptions."

It was then I noted the accent. She was a transplant. New York, maybe Jersey. The woman with the bun came back with ice water for me, and an espresso for Almondson.

"So, you were trying to remember who you represent," Almondson said.

"Yes. Did you know that some of your staff have received death threats?"

She frowned, presenting no visible wrinkles, which I figured made frowning kind of pointless. "Death threats? I've heard no such thing. And I'm on the floor every night."

"You make it into the fronton?"

She leaned back in her chair with her little coffee cup. "Ah, the jai alai."

"You don't like jai alai?"

"Honestly, its not my kind of game, no. But it is part of who we are, and I like the guys. They work hard. So you say someone is threatening them?"

I nodded. "The pelotari have been drumming up some PR. Seems someone doesn't like that."

"You have picked up the lingua franca quickly, haven't you?" she said.

"What makes you think I'm not a life long jai alai fan?"

"If you were a fan, you would come to see the performances, and if you'd come to the performances, I'd remember you."

"You remember everyone who comes through your casino?"

She shook her head slowly. "Only the ones worth remembering." She sipped her coffee. "So tell me about these threats."

"Your security isn't very good here, you know that?"

"I know good help is hard to find, but why do you say that?"

"You've got a very impressive looking fellow manning the elevators downstairs. But I told him I had an appointment with you, when I didn't. And I called you Mr. Almondson, neither of which bothered him a bit."

Almondson leaned forward and made a note on a pad and spoke as she did. "Like I say, good help is hard to find."

"The pelotari received death threats, left in their lockers. What kind of security is that?"

She leaned back in her chair and looked at me. I saw her eyes move, up and down, then side to side, like it was her turn to inspect me. "There's no money in the fronton, so it doesn't have the same security level," she said. "Having said that, if someone is getting into the locker room, that's unacceptable. I'll see things are tightened up down there."

"That would be a start. But it doesn't explain why the threats are coming at all."

"I don't know what to tell you, Mr. Jones. Things are tense right now, with the Compact due for renegotiation. The Seminole would like to see the backs of us, as would any number of the other pari-mutuels. A lot of the racetracks are struggling. One less competitor would suit them nicely."

"But why threaten the pelotari?"

Almondson looked away, giving the question some thought. She made thinking look good.

"I guess," she said, returning her eyes to me, "because they are an easy target. They are not covered by the same security or regulation as workers on the casino floor. Perhaps they are a way to hurt the casino without drawing so much attention."

"But to what end?" I said. "I mean, let's say the threats succeed and jai alai gets shut down. I've been out there, Miss Almondson; it's not exactly a full house. Would there really be any impact to the casino?"

She smiled. "It's Ms. Almondson." I nodded in apology and she continued. "But you can call me Jenny. And the effect, Mr. Jones, would be catastrophic. No jai alai means no casino. We are a pari-mutuel. That means jai alai is our *raison d'être*. The gaming laws say we cannot have a casino without the fronton."

I nodded as I recalled Eric Edwards explaining that to me, but now I realized how inextricably linked the two parts were. We sat watching each other for a moment, a game that I knew I was going to lose, so I stood.

"Thank you for your time, Jenny. I trust you'll look into the security issues in the fronton."

"I shall attend to it this morning, Mr. Jones," she said, standing and gliding around her desk.

"Call me Miami," I said.

She nodded and the earring shone across her smooth neck. "That's an interesting name, Miami. Were you born there?" she said, walking me to the door.

"No, it was a college thing that just sort of stuck. How about you? You didn't go to school here."

"No, Princeton."

"How many months have you been here?"

"Six. Is it that obvious?"

I smiled. "You don't look Florida."

"I'm sorry I don't meet your approval," she said with a half grin.

"I assure you, it wasn't a criticism."

We walked out to the main lobby, and she hit the elevator button.

"You like it here?" I said, making waiting-for-the-elevator small talk.

"I like winter."

"Yeah, summers can be brutal. You should get out on the water. You'd love it."

The elevator dinged, and I stepped in.

"Is that an invitation?" she said.

"It would be, if I had a boat."

"But you don't."

"No," I said.

She cocked an eyebrow as the door slid closed between us.

"That's a shame."

CHAPTER TEN

I found Ron at the fronton, watching the pelotari warming up. Ron sat about halfway back, but there wasn't a soul in front of him.

"How goes it, Mr. Bennett?"

He looked up at me and blinked hard, like he'd been a million miles away.

"Discover anything?" I said.

Ron shook his head as I sat down. "I have just walked through pretty much every area that took my fancy," he said. "There might be some big boys out there for show on the casino floor, but there's nobody gives a hoot outside that. I just waltzed into the locker room behind the jai alai here. A janitor even gave me a wink."

I shook my head, and we turned to look at the court. Julio was rotating his arm over, whipping the ball against the granite wall.

"This used to be quite the place, you know," said Ron.

"You've been here before?"

Ron let out a soft snort. "I used to come to the fronton all the time. I met my first wife here."

"You don't say."

He nodded. "Back in the late seventies, boy this was the place to come. The one down in Miami was bigger; that was amazing. But even here in West Palm. People used to come from the island, slumming it in West Palm, just to be seen at the jai alai. Everyone who was anyone was here. President Ford was here once, famous sportsmen, celebrities."

He turned and pointed at the darkened box behind us. "See there? That was the skybox where the celebs sat, the ones that didn't want to mingle with the common folk. But that was the thing about the jai alai. It didn't matter whether you were famous or not, rich or poor. Everyone came, all together."

He smiled at the thought, and I saw the silver hair and sun-bleached face go back in time.

"There was a restaurant up in the box, with a chef from some five-star place. Really good food. I met Janice here in the stands." He looked at me. "She was so young and so full of life. The pace of the jai alai had nothing on her. Anyway, I proposed in that restaurant. Just a kid I was, asking the love of his life for her hand."

"And she said yes?"

"Unfortunately, yes." He let out a laugh and slapped my shoulder. "There was a dress code, did you know? Everyone looked so smart. Jackets, ties, cocktails dresses, the whole nine yards. Everyone was so beautiful. The seats here were bleachers back then. They reached high up to the back, not floor level like they are now. Rows of hats all the way up and cigar smoke that clung to the ceiling like a fog. On a big night there could be ten thousand people in here. Now the fire department would never allow it."

He looked around the empty seating area. "Even if people still wanted to come."

"There's something I don't get," I said. "So Julio there. Why does his playing jersey say twenty-five on the back but four on the front?"

Ron nodded. "Twenty-five is his player number at the fronton. He's always that number. But four is his position in the order of play. That can change every day."

I nodded, and we sat listening to the ball echo off the wall.

"That sound, the pelota, brings back memories."

"The what?"

"The pelota, the thing they're throwing."

"I just thought that was a ball."

Ron shook his head. "No," he said, looking around as if searching for something. "I wonder if they're still here."

Ron stood and waved for me to follow. We edged along the row of seats, then out to an open area where some of the pelotari were stretching. I got a few smiles and nods, which I returned. We wandered around the back of the skybox to an open door. A set of tight stairs led up, and Ron just started up as if it were his house. They were steep, almost like a ladder. At the top, Ron stopped and knocked, then entered.

We stepped into a room that must have doubled as a time machine. Two men sat in front of a swamp cooler, and an old television replayed a *Roseanne* episode that neither of the men looked at. Each man must have been sixty, but they were as different as people get. One man was thin and bore some Asian heritage, maybe Filipino. He had an ageless face, tanned hard, with a toothless smile. He was hand weaving the scoop-like baskets that the pelotari attached to their hands to fling the pelota at the wall. The other man, larger, with olive skin and a heavy brow, was Spanish at a guess. He appeared to be making the balls, or pelotas. The laugh track went off on the *Roseanne* episode and the men both laughed, apparently at the laugh track, not the gag.

"This man is making the cesta, the basket they use to catch the pelota," said Ron. "He hand cuts these reeds, and then shapes and weaves them into the scoop shape."

I watched the old man at work, scraping at a long thin reed with a piece of broken glass. Then Ron drew my attention to the other man.

"He is making the pelota," he said. "They're made from rubber, latex and goatskin."

"I wouldn't have thought there would be much call for pelotas these days," I said.

"Well, each pelota only lasts about twenty minutes before it cracks. And they're worth about a hundred bucks apiece."

"Wow, makes golf look cheap," I said.

We stood watching the men for a time. There were all kinds of metal implements hanging on the walls. It looked like a torture chamber. But the men seemed content to work in silence, with mostly their hands and cut glass. Ron tapped my shoulder, and we wandered out and back down the stairs.

"That was something," I said.

Ron nodded as we made our way back to the seating.

"So what happened?" I said. "If this game was such hot stuff, how did it end up like this?"

Ron let out a sigh and sat, eyes on the brightly lit court. "Lots of things I guess. More competition for sure. The NBA arrived, the MLB, even NHL. All big sports with TV coverage. ESPN doesn't even show jai alai on its Internet channel. Plus there was the big strike."

"The big strike?"

"Yeah, back in eighty-eight. A huge players' strike. It went on for three years, more or less. A lot of bad blood, inferior players came in, and the crowds walked out. NBA had just started a team in Miami in eighty-eight, and the Marlins brought Major League Baseball to South Florida in ninety-three."

"Hard to believe in less than thirty years it's become this," I said, looking around the near-empty stands as the announcer warmed up and the first two players took the court.

"Believe it," said Ron. "It's the way of the world. Nations never think they'll change, empires never think they'll fall, but they always do. Sports are the same. It doesn't take too much to see it happening. Take football. NFL is the most popular game in the country by a mile, in terms of viewers and supporters. But it has faced strikes before, and they hurt it. Well imagine a big strike— a season or two off, or with lesser players. Then add in rule changes, because of all the head clashes and suspected brain damage. Suddenly, the game has less appeal and people take their support elsewhere. Football is already dropping in terms of participation. Soccer is booming." He shrugged. "The way of the world."

"Well, it sounded like a good time, while it lasted."

Ron smiled. "It was the best time. I'll never forget it. Neither will anyone who was there. It was just one of those times, one of those places."

Again he looked into middle distance and drifted away. I wondered if he was thinking about being young, of having his whole life ahead of him, of crowds and noise and the crush of youth. Of young love and asking a girl for marriage for the first time, and the life ahead, and of all that meant.

Ron drifted back and turned to me. "What about you?. Mr. Almondson, was it?"

"Mister is actually Ms. And quite the package at that."

"Did you keep your mind on the job?"

"About as much as usual, but she seems like a smart operator. I'm not surprised you found the security wanting. It was the same in the admin area. She says she'll tighten that up, so we'll see. I think the players will be safe enough, at work at least."

We watched the performance for a while, listening to the pelota crack on the granite walls and echo around the room like a memory. Then I turned and saw Lucas ambling into the fronton. He nodded in our direction.

"Is that Lucas?" said Ron.

"Yup."

"What's he doing up here?"

"We have to see a man about a bet," I said, pulling a cell phone out of my pocket and sending a text message to a number I didn't know.

CHAPTER ELEVEN

When Lucas heard the intel about the bookie's van I had gotten from El Tiburon, aka Brandon, he said he wanted in. He was taking the whole thing with Desi to heart, so much so that I wondered what was behind it, but regardless there was no talking him out of it. He said whoever was at the top of the tree was as responsible for Desi as the two drunks that tossed him in the water, and he wasn't letting another kid get tossed in the drink. Or worse. We left Ron to his reverie and wandered out into the daylight. The sunshine burned white after the artificial twilight of the casino, and we squinted to adjust our eyes.

"You sent the message?" said Lucas.

"Just as the kid said."

"El Tiburon." Lucas laughed. "Kids. They really think they are indestructible."

"Were you any different?"

"Nah, mate, not at all. But I didn't call myself the Shark."

"I gotta say though, I can totally see you carrying that off," I said.

Lucas smiled and shook his head. "You're having a lend of yourself, mate."

We walked around the building to the spot where we had our little altercation with the big Irish lugnuts on our first visit. There were still dark stains on patches of gravel, where the big boys had leaked some blood. I felt butterflies in my stomach. I'm not afraid of confrontation; there are very few good pitchers who are. But they say Jack Lemmon threw up from nerves before every performance, and that boy could act. It was the unknown that got in my guts, playing the scenarios out before they ever happened. It was wasted energy, and I didn't like wasting effort, but I had felt it before every game I ever threw, and I felt it now. I reconciled myself with the fact that it meant I was still alive. Lucas on the other hand, looked like he had settled in for the afternoon. He was relaxed against the wall, hands slack by his side, eyes staring at nothing in particular.

My mentor and friend Lenny Cox had met Lucas somewhere in his travels. Where and how I had never heard, but Lenny had always played his cards pretty close. I knew he had done something for the National Security Agency, and before that, some kind of special forces, Marines or Army Rangers or some such. He never really got into the details. Lucas had served in a similar capacity in the Australian Defense Force, the SAS maybe. Suffice it to say they had both seen and done things they didn't care to talk about, and a lot of important people preferred they kept to themselves. Somewhere along the line, Lenny had done something that involved saving Lucas's family, and Lucas had forever considered himself in Lenny's debt.

"You been to see Lenny, lately?" I asked Lucas.

Lucas opened an eye and shook his head. "Not in a while. I need to get down there."

"Me too. I was thinking maybe we should drop by after this."

Lucas kicked himself away from the wall and looked past me. "Sounds good," he said. "Looks like we're on."

I turned to see a red delivery van approaching. It was the sort of thing that delivered fruit and vegetables, or dry cleaning, and it raced across the parking lot and skidded to a stop in front of us. The door slid open on the side, revealing two guys, plus the driver.

"Get in," said the guy operating the door. He was a short Mexican with a barrel chest and a black tank top. I stepped up and into the rear of the van. Two rows of bench seats were inside and Lucas followed me in. The little Mexican slid the door home and the driver hit the gas as he heard it sliding. We pulled around the building and out onto surface streets, headed under the freeway. The third guy looked like the main man. Apart from the fact that he wasn't actually doing any of the work, he wore the casual arrogance of someone who considers himself the boss—even if that consisted of riding around in a beat up delivery van all day.

The driver pulled onto one of the roads around the airport, and the boss man turned to us in the back. He had tattoos on his neck that moved when he spoke. They were just random lines to me, but they seemed to dance when he moved his jaw, and it made me smile.

"What the hell you smiling at?" he said.

"Your tattoos."

"You think my tats are funny?" he said, brushing open his shirt to reveal a handgun tucked into his jeans at the hip.

"We got business or what?" said Lucas.

"You better tell your *amigo* to mind hisself," said boss man.

"He don't mean nothing. So where we going?"

Boss man smiled. "We ain't going nowhere, bro. This is the office, right here."

Lucas smiled back. "No, seriously mate. We need to speak to the main man."

"As far as you concerned, I'm the main man."

"You're a delivery boy bouncing around in a fruit van, if the smell is anything to go by. I'm talking about the actual main man."

Boss man ground his teeth at Lucas. "How you know El Tiburon?" he snarled.

"I never met the guy," said Lucas. "But he sounds like a right drongo."

"He what?" said boss man.

"I met him at Los Piños," I interjected.

"You?" he said, looking me up and down. "What the hell you doing at Los Piños?"

"Last time, as I recall, I was kicking the living daylights out of the Shark."

The two guys looked at me like I'd just invited them to solve an anti-differential equation. I could almost see the smoke coming off their heads as the gears spun around. Then boss man made like he was going for his handgun.

Lucas kicked out his foot, striking the lever that folded the seats down, and the two guys flopped backwards at us. Before the seat back had even settled in the down position, Lucas gave both guys a karate chop on the back of the neck, and they fell limp.

"They're not dead, are they?" I said.

Lucas shook his head. "Not yet," he smiled. "That'd be no fun."

Lucas grabbed the gun that was sticking out of boss man's jeans and pointed it at the driver's head.

"Up ahead by the airport you're gonna come to a bunch of noise barriers. Pull in behind them," said Lucas.

The driver could see his prone comrades and made the smart play. He pulled behind the sound barriers. I slid out of the van on the driver's side and helped the driver out, then took the keys. Lucas kept the gun on the driver the whole time, then jumped out himself.

"How's your day going so far?" asked Lucas.

The driver was a big guy, round in all the wrong places. He didn't look like anyone's idea of a hero. "Look I don't got no money. I don't handle that," he said.

"Don't want your money, hoss. Just need to know where the boss man hangs out," said Lucas.

The driver looked toward the boss man lying on the collapsed seat.

"Not that fella, the real boss man. *El Jefe*," said Lucas.

The driver shook his head as his eyes shifted left and right.

"Think hard, dopey. See your two Irish buddies from the fronton, they took some money that didn't belong to them and then tried to kill a little boy. *El Niño.*"

"You beat those guys?" said the guy, wide-eyed.

Lucas raised an eyebrow. "Yeah, so we need to have a word with El Jefe about how he goes about his business."

"I don't know, man. I don't know."

Lucas could jot down on the inside of a matchbook more about fighting and dispensing pain than I would ever know. Hitting people was an occupational requirement, but it wasn't something I particularly enjoyed or felt competent in. But one thing I did know was the human body. A baseball season is like a war. A long, arduous series of battles, day after day, each one with the potential to put you in harm's way. Baseball players know a lot about where a body is going to break down, where its failure points are. Back then, learning about that had helped keep me on the field. Now, understanding the body's vulnerabilities aided me in a completely different way.

"You see that knee you're leaning on there, pal?" I said.

The guy looked down at his own leg.

"Yeah, at your weight, that thing goes backwards, it's gonna snap like a twig and you're gonna spend the rest of your days scooting around in one of those electric wheelchairs. You got three seconds to decide if you want to talk or you want to be hobbled."

The guy made his mind up pretty quick. He set his jaw firm, like a child zipping his lips and throwing away the key.

"One," I said.

The driver glared at me through the little slits he called eyes.

"Two."

A snarl formed on his lips.

"Three."

He tensed for the hit. It was the worst thing he could have done. He put more weight on the left leg, and stiffened, meaning it was going to snap instead of bend. I kept him hanging, not moving, then I looked at Lucas. The driver glanced at Lucas, as well. Lucas just raised his eyebrows again, as if to say, *some folks is just too dumb to help*.

I kicked my foot out like I was in the windup for a fastball, and before the driver had the chance to look away from Lucas, I cracked my boot into the guy's kneecap. It popped with an audible crack, one half slipping around the outside, the other around the inside of his knee. His considerable girth drove down as the knee buckled backwards and ripped all the tendons away from the bone. I'd seem some seriously nasty knee injuries playing college football, but this one took the cake. It was pretty much every knee injury in the book, all in one go.

The driver hit the ground with a dull thud, and his scream was lost in the wash of a jet taking off in the direction of the Bahamas. The poor guy tried to grab at his knee, but he wasn't near flexible enough, so he ended up groping at nothing but air while his leg stuck out at the most unnatural of directions.

Lucas stepped over and put his boot into the guy's shoulder. "You still got another knee there, champ. You wanna go again?"

The driver shook his head vigorously and, through tears, gave us an address on Okeechobee Boulevard. As the driver lay there, Lucas and I pulled the other two guys out of the van and laid them next to their chauffeur.

"All right mate, I don't fancy walkin' all that way back, so we're gonna take your van for a bit. We'll leave it at the casino for you to collect, okay?"

Lucas gave the guy a mouthful of teeth that shone from his deeply tanned face, and we left them there to consider their sins.

CHAPTER TWELVE

Lucas and I considered our own sins, with a six-pack, sitting on the grass in the cemetery. Lucas popped the top on one and passed it to me, then opened another, which he placed against the headstone. The third he kept for himself. We clinked all three bottles together and took a long pull, then Lucas picked up the bottle by the VA-supplied headstone and poured the contents into the ground.

"Cheers, Lenny," said Lucas.

I held my beer up in salute. "To Lenny."

"Lenny," said Lucas. He took another slug of beer. "I sure do miss the old mongrel."

I smiled. "Me too. He taught me everything worth knowing. Outside of baseball, that is." I took another sip. "How did you guys meet, exactly?"

"Oh, it was a long time ago," said Lucas. "In a galaxy far away, as they say. I could tell ya, but then I'd have to kill ya. And you're too good a bloke for that."

"Cheers."

"I will tell you one thing, Miami. We did a lot of stuff, me and Lenny—stuff that wasn't real flash. Don't get me wrong, it was stuff that needed doing, and I'd do most of it again, but still. We did some things that aren't conducive to a good night's sleep. But Lenny never did anything for selfish means. Not for his own gain. He helped a lot of people. Me included. You too."

I nodded. "Got that right. After my dad died, when I was at college, I could have gone either way. I got lucky meeting Lenny."

"Lotta people would say that. He paid it forward, old Lenny. He did one for me, saved my family once. Nasty business, but he was there, and he saved them. And you know he never asked for nothing in return. Not ever, not once."

"But you felt a debt?" I said.

"I guess." He shrugged. "How could you not?"

"I get it. But you know, that debt doesn't extend to me."

"What makes you say that?" he said, sipping his beer.

"You're always there, just like Lenny was. I sometimes think you help me out because you feel indebted to me. Because of him, somehow."

Lucas smiled. "Geez, you're a dill. I don't feel any debt to you. That's not it at all, mate. Just like we're saying about Lenny. It's about paying it forward. I help because I can, not because I have to or feel indebted. Just 'cause I can. That's the best thing Lenny taught, and the silly bugger didn't even know he was doing it. Pay it forward. Give someone a hand, so maybe they'll do the same for someone else, someday."

I nodded and smiled, then stuck my beer in my mouth. It was the most talkative I'd ever heard Lucas, and I wondered if he didn't do most of his talking at Lenny's gravesite.

"What happened to your family, Lucas? You never really mention them."

He nodded and frowned. "Well, I'm not the easiest bugger to live with."

"Who of us is?"

"Yeah, but the life I've lived, its not one you get past. It's who you are. And that makes it hard. My missus, she's a lovely girl. A real beauty. We had two little ones, although they're not so little anymore. And she wanted what people want for their kids, you know? A house, a lawn, schools, picnics, all that."

He shrugged and took a long pull at his beer. "Anyway, she knew that wasn't something I was capable of. So she left. No harsh words or nothing. She just upped sticks back to Oz, and that was that. She's been remarried a long time now, so that was the right call."

He finished his beer, then opened three more, and poured one onto Lenny's grave. He didn't seem melancholy, just matter of fact. I finished my beer and took the second and sipped at it, wondering if I were capable of the things Lucas was not. A house, a lawn, school, picnics, all that. Lucas interrupted that train of thought.

"Best knock this one off and head back to Miami. Got a party boat going out of the marina tonight. Some Russian mob."

"The Russian mob?"

"No, mate, not *the* Russian mob, *a* Russian mob. A group of Russians. Geez, what language do you fellas talk?"

I smiled and took a long pull on my beer. "What about our bookmaker friend? Think I should stop by?"

"Nah, I wanna be there for that. Besides, do him good to stew for a while. Think about his life for a bit, knowing we're out there. You know?"

I nodded. I knew.

CHAPTER THIRTEEN

The breeze had dropped off, and the evening was postcard perfect when I got back to Singer Island. After my chat with Lucas, I was glad to see Danielle's car in the drive. I stepped in through the front door to the scent of lime and the roar of the blender.

"Perfect timing, as usual," she smiled. "I felt like a margarita. Want one?"

"Is that a trick question?"

We settled into our loungers overlooking the Intracoastal. Some kind of race was in the making, as a flotilla of yachts drifted past.

"How was your day?" she asked.

"Eventful."

"Do I want to know?" she said, raising an eyebrow. It was not the kind of look she should be giving if she wanted me to behave.

"I've been hired by some jai alai players who are getting death threats."

"jai alai? They still play that?"

"They do."

"And death threats. Did they contact the West Palm PD?"

"I don't know. I doubt it."

"Why do all these people complain about crimes not getting solved, but then never report anything?"

"I don't think this is your complaining crowd. Anyway, how was your day?"

Danielle edged off her lounger and stood. "More margarita?" she asked.

"Sure."

She wandered inside, and I watched her all the way. She moved like river water across rocks, and I could watch it like other folks watched television.

"I got steaks out for dinner," she called from the kitchen.

"Red meat steaks?"

"Yes."

"Not fake soy steaks?"

"No," she smiled, coming back out and handing me my drink. "I just felt like steak."

"Okay," I said, letting sleeping dogs lie. "So you were saying, your day?"

"Interesting also. I got asked to go to a conference."

"A conference? What sort of conference."

"What sort do you think? A law enforcement conference. Leadership in Modern Law Enforcement," she said, air quoting the name of the event.

"All right, leadership. That sounds good. Where is it?"

"Atlanta."

"Hotlanta? Nice," I said, licking salt from my lips.

"You think?"

"Well, I've never actually been to Atlanta, but I hear it's all right."

"No, I mean about the conference."

"Definitely. Sounds like a hell of an opportunity."

"That's what I thought when the boss asked. He was supposed to go but something came up, so he offered it to me."

"That's great that he's thinking about you like that," I said.

"Like what?"

"Like a leader, I guess."

She nodded and took a sip. "I've never really thought about it, not really. I mean, what's after this? I don't want to be a patrol deputy all my life, do I? But I never really thought about myself in a leadership role, heading a team. It's a different challenge."

"It is, for sure. So when is this thing?"

She took the straw from her mouth and stirred her drink. "That's the thing. I have to leave tomorrow."

"Tomorrow? That's not a lot of notice."

"No, but like I said, the boss was supposed to go and can't. I'm worried if I say no, I might not get another chance like this."

"No, absolutely, you should go. No reason not to."

"I think it will be good for me to get away for a while, you know? I'm actually really excited. I guess that's a bit silly, but I haven't felt this excited about anything for a while."

I grinned and winked, and she let go a killer smile. Then she stood again.

"I'll get those steaks ready."

Danielle sauntered inside, and I called out to ask if she needed help. She told me no, to just chill out. So that's what I did. Except I wasn't chilling. I was wondering why she hadn't felt excited about anything lately. All that had happened was that we had moved in together. No biggie. Or, more precisely, I had moved her in. Danielle had received a gunshot wound from a drug dealer only a few months earlier. As fate would have it, she hadn't been on duty or in pursuit of the guy. He'd actually been trying to get at me. Her townhouse had been damaged in the gunfire, then got turned into a crime scene, so I moved her in with me. When it came time for her to move back to her place, she didn't. And that was just fine and dandy with me.

But I couldn't help feeling there was a lot going on behind those eyes. Getting shot could really mess with your priorities, and lately I couldn't get a fix on where Danielle's lay. I had the sense we were treading water,

waiting for the shark to burst through the surface, or not.
I had to admit I was pretty damned happy. Work was
good, I had great drinking buddies down at Longboard
Kelly's, and I came home to the most wonderful woman
I'd ever known. She could kick my backside in a sit-up
competition, then do the same in Trivial Pursuit. She was
a confident, capable sheriff's deputy, with a heart of
something a hell of a lot more worthy than gold.

Even watching her with Desi, when Lucas had
brought the boy to our house. The kid had only
responded to her, not me or Lucas. And it wasn't some
professional skill. It was caring. Maybe that's what Lucas
was trying to say, in his way. Paying it forward was just
another way of saying caring, and Danielle had that in
spades. She had looked after me, more than once, when
I'd been laid up after some altercation or other, and I
couldn't help think, maybe she was looking for someone
to care about. And now, living with me, she had realized
that I didn't need caring for. That maybe I was like Lucas.
A difficult bugger to live with.

I resolved that encouraging her to go to Atlanta was
the right thing to do. I further resolved to be there when
she got back—really be there. Not just be a body on the
next lounger, but really listen to what she was saying—
about the shooting, about her dreams, about where she
wanted to go. And as I sat looking at the sunset falling
behind the Everglades, I hoped like hell that I was actually
capable of all that I resolved.

CHAPTER FOURTEEN

The Hard Rock Casino near Fort Lauderdale Airport had so little in common with the West Palm Jai Alai and Casino that it was hard to even call them the same species. The Hard Rock empire had been purchased by the Seminole tribe some years ago for close on a billion dollars—proof enough if anyone needed it that the tribe was doing mighty fine from its concessions across the state. The Lauderdale version had become one of the largest casino resorts in the world. The auditorium space alone held over five thousand fans, and all by itself attracted more customers than the jai alai in West Palm by a factor close to a thousand.

I wandered through the casino floor, the bells and buzzers and artificial noise of the slots permeating every corner of the place. The rattle and clink of coins dropping on a jackpot was no more, as the vast majority of slots were electronic and dropped your winnings, in a most unromantic fashion, onto a plastic card.

I knew from previous experience that security at the Hard Rock was a step or ten up from the West Palm Jai Alai, so I didn't try any funny stuff to weasel my way past these chunky guards. I just called up, lied my keister off, and made an appointment. I dropped every name I could think off. Some, like Eric Edwards and the governor, would not be happy about being used as pawns, but they would just have to learn to live with it.

The offices of Jackie Bass overlooked the massive pool complex that wound its way through the lush gardens of the hotel. His private elevator was guarded by a massive Seminole, the kind of guy you could actually envisage wrestling an alligator. He checked me out, gave me a pat down, then deposited me at reception. A young Seminole woman took my name and asked if I wanted water. I didn't wait long. It seemed Mr. Bass was a pretty punctual guy. He was also filthy rich. Indian gaming had been good for a lot of tribes around the country, bringing in money to previously dirt-poor communities. But along the way, it had also made the tribal elders boatloads of cash. And being a sovereign nation, not only were they exempt from tax, but they also didn't have to share their financial accounts with anyone. Accusations of dirty deals were as regular as carols at Christmas, but no one seemed to give a damn.

Jackie Bass wore a disarming smile and a suit that was halfway between Saville Row and Osceola, a gray suit jacket with white shirt, and a neckpiece of beads and feathers. His hair was jet black, tied back, and his face was well weathered in the way of his people.

"Mr. Jones," he said, shaking my hand. "How do you like our little establishment?"

"I'm not much of a gambler, I'm afraid."

Bass smiled and winked. "Me neither."

The woman who had shown me in placed a glass of water on a coffee table for me. It seemed everyone had both a desk and a meeting table in their office these days, and I wondered if there was some kind of logic between which one a person chose to meet you at. I stood by the huge tinted window, looking over the pool.

"Amazing, isn't it?"

I nodded. It was. So much chlorinated water and fake rockwork, only a few miles from one of the most beautiful beaches on the planet.

"Do you swim, Mr. Bass?"

He gave a chuckle and moved away from the window toward the coffee table. "Not in that pool. You know how many people urinate in that thing? I'd rather swim in a toilet."

He smiled again and gestured for me to take a seat.

"So you mentioned to my assistant something about a PR disaster in the making?"

"With the Compact being negotiated again, I thought you'd want to know."

"And I appreciate that." He leaned back in his chair and brushed his lapels.

"Do you know the Jai Alai and Casino in West Palm?" I said.

Bass nodded. "Never been in it, but I know it."

"The jai alai players are getting death threats."

Bass frowned and considered this. "That's not good. I hope the police find whoever is doing it. But I don't see the connection with us."

I sipped some water before replying. "Well, some people think that the competition might be trying to squeeze the casino. And some people might see that competition as you."

Bass smiled again. I was either funny as hell, or way off-base, at least in his mind. "Competition? Mr. Jones, we are one of the elite casinos of the world. Our competition is in Las Vegas or Macau or Monaco."

I raised a mental eyebrow at Monaco but let him continue.

"No offense to them, but the pari-mutuels are small fry, little establishments for a class of guest that the tribe is not really interested in catering to."

"Word is that the legislature are considering killing the Compact, offering expansion to the pari-mutuels. That would make them competitors, would it not?"

"If that were to happen, maybe. But our people in Tallahassee tell us there is no mood there to change the Compact. The politicians know, as we do, that if they remove our exclusive rights to slots and other conditions, then we owe the state of Florida nothing. Nothing, Mr. Jones. Our current agreement offers a minimum of one billion dollars over five years. It would be a brave legislature that tosses that income out the window in favor of the greyhounds and jai alai."

He smiled again. He was pretty confident in his theory, and I suspected there were some well connected and highly paid folks giving him his intel. But I also knew that as a bloc, the pari-mutuels also had support in Tallahassee and, Compact or not, could make the fight harder than the Seminole might want it to be.

"Mr. Jones, I appreciate your concern, but I see no PR issue. This problem is a great distance from us. We put hundreds of millions into the state, we create thousands of Florida jobs, and we bring many millions more into the economy simply by being here. We are no threat to these mom-and-pop operations, and they are none to us."

I nodded but stayed silent. It all made sense. Maybe too much sense. I stood.

"Mr. Bass, I thank you for you time."

"Mr. Jones, I'm glad you stopped by. Lily will give you a gaming credit on your way out, if you like. Try some of the new slots."

"Like I said, Mr. Bass, I don't gamble."

Bass smiled again.

"You'd be playing with my money, Mr. Jones. That's not gambling. That's a sure thing."

CHAPTER FIFTEEN

I left the Seminole casino and drove a short distance west under the turnpike flyover. The apartment building was in a cluster of similar buildings built west of Hollywood, by a property investment company headed by Seminole Chief James Kowechobe. Jackie Bass sat on the board of directors. Although the property sat outside tribal lands, most of the tenants were Seminole. Because of their national sovereignty, Native Americans who lived on tribal lands were not subject to state tax, so in many states the tribal members kept close to home. But because there was no state tax in Florida, the incentive to live on tribal land was effectively zero, save the subsidized housing. The tribal elders building low-cost housing on state land was seen by many as another gesture of support for the tribe. Others saw it as the tribe keeping its manipulative claws around its people. I wasn't sure which was true.

I pulled the Escape into the shade of a royal palm and took the steps up, two at a time. On the second level was the apartment I sought.

Jimmy Tigerfoot smiled broadly when he saw me and leaped into a bear hug that rendered my arms useless. He was dark and muscular and had no need of a shirt.

"Miami, come in. It's been too long."

I stepped into the cool apartment. It was a three bedroom, with a small living–dining area, and a decent enough kitchen, from which Jimmy's wife, Petal, came in and hugged me. I knew Petal wasn't her real Seminole name, but I also knew something about losing your birth name somewhere along life's journey.

"How are you, Miami?" she said, joy lifting the corner of her eyes.

"I'm well. Very well. And you guys? How are the boys?"

"School," said Jimmy. "Doing well. Thanks to you."

I shook my head. "Will you forget that? It's done. Their success is because you guys are great parents, not anything I did."

The two of them glanced at each other like I was a lunatic, then let it drop.

"You want an iced tea, Miami?" said Petal.

"Love one," I said, settling on the sofa with Jimmy. "How's work?"

"Good, good," said Jimmy. "There's lots of tourists want to learn to surf, so we're pretty busy, especially this time of year."

"Many still think you're Hawaiian?" I smiled.

Jimmy laughed. "At least one a day. But the Hard Rock doesn't say *Indian Casino* on the door, so why should they know? What about you?"

"Busy too. Just been to see Jackie Bass, actually."

"Ooh, the boss man. What are you doing with the tribe?"

"Nothing. I've got a client from one of those small casinos in West Palm. You know the jai alai?"

"They still play that?"

"They do, some. Anyway, he's getting threats, so I'm checking it out."

"You think the Seminole are involved?"

"I don't know, Jimmy. Just turning over rocks right now. What do you think? Jackie Bass says he pays no attention to the pari-mutuels. Says they're small-time."

Petal brought iced tea in and sat with us. "They're no Hard Rock, but as a group they are getting some attention," she said.

"Yeah, I don't think Jackie is being one hundred percent upfront with you there," said Jimmy. "He's a sharp operator. He watches everyone."

"That's what I thought. So tell me this. He says the Compact is too good a deal for the state for them to walk away. But what about the tribe? Is it good for the tribe?"

"I'll tell you who it's good for. It's good for Jackie Bass. The Chief, too," said Jimmy.

"Yeah I saw the chief's new waterfront *chickee*," I said. "Nice boat there."

"Jimmy's right," said Petal. "The leaders have made a lot of money since the tribe started the casinos. But the tribal members have benefited, too. Every member of the tribe gets a monthly stipend from the casino profits. Before the casinos, most Seminole lived in poverty. Now we have real homes, money for education. And since the Compact came in, the stipend has gone up. We are a family of four, and we all get the stipend, even the boys. Really, we don't have to work if we don't want to. But we want our boys to grow up independent, to not rely on handouts that might end. So the stipend has been good but also bad. Many Seminole have alcohol problems, and there are drugs. Sitting around all day doing nothing is not how we are supposed to operate."

I nodded and sipped some tea. "Bass said they create a lot of jobs. Don't those go to tribe members?"

"Mostly," said Jimmy. "If you want to work, you can. But not every Seminole wants to work in a casino, right? Even me, I get most of my business through the casino hotel, and they don't ask for a cut, because I am a tribe member. I don't want to work in the casino, but I do want to work."

"Yeah, surfing all day, that's a real chore."

He smiled. "Life is what you make it, brother."

"What's your gut, then? Would the elders be involved in threats to my client?"

"My gut says at the top, no," said Jimmy. "Those guys move in the big circle, right? They deal with the governor and all that. But there are guys—the ones at the bottom

—maybe want to make a name for themselves. It has happened before, guys doing dumb things to get noticed by the casino board or the tribal council."

"There are always rogue elements in any community, aren't there?" added Petal. "But the council, I don't think they're into that. Like Jimmy says, this is a big-stakes game now. It's won or lost in the corridors of power in Tallahassee, not in the back streets of Fort Lauderdale, or even West Palm."

"Thanks, guys. You've been a big help."

"We owe you, brother," said Jimmy.

I shook my head. "You're never gonna quit on that, are you."

"Nope," he said, smiling.

"Then there's something I want from you."

"Name it," he said.

I looked at Petal. "Last time I saw you, you made these little taco things."

"Indian tacos," smiled Jimmy. "No curry required," he laughed and slapped his thighs.

Petal smiled, too.

"And I was just about to make some lunch," she said. "You sit tight."

CHAPTER SIXTEEN

I enjoyed lunch with Jimmy and Petal, then headed back home to collect Danielle. We drove in silence to Palm Beach International for her flight to Atlanta. PBI was one of those airports that was certainly bigger than an airfield, but didn't carry the stress of the huge airports like LAX or MIA or JFK. I stopped by the curb and got Danielle's case out of the trunk. I gave her a hug like she was heading off for a tour of duty, and she kissed me hard. An airport police officer came near, but instead of telling us to move on, he just smiled.

"I'll call when I get there," Danielle said.

I nodded and watched her saunter into the terminal, doing for jeans and a plain white shirt exactly what the designer intended. When she was gone I slipped back into the Escape and headed for Longboard Kelly's. Before I met Danielle it had been more my home than my home, and even now it was a refuge. As I walked in the rear entrance to the courtyard, a sense of calm came over me. The tables with their beer-labeled umbrellas, the palapa-style roof over the outdoor bar, even the surfboard with the bite out of it hanging on the back fence. They were to me like Florida in general was for the tourists. I saw their faces and watched their expressions, as they deplaned or stretched their weary legs beside Winnebagos. I saw the stress of whatever their real life involved evaporate as the sun and the sea and the thought of a cool drink with a lime wedge stole them away. That's how I felt walking into Longboard Kelly's.

Even better when Ron waited for me on his stool at the palapa bar. Muriel stood behind the bar, in her usual tank top despite the cooler weather, indifferent to the goose bumps on her arms. She poured me a beer before I reached my stool, then leaned back against the bar on the other side, the side that served those customers who preferred to sit indoors.

She thrust her more than ample bosom at me. "If it ain't Miami Jones. Where have you been, stranger?"

I took the beer and threw half of it back in one go. "Out earning a living, sadly," I said. "But I am all the better for seeing you."

She looked at Ron. "They all love me, because I serve beer."

"There is no truer love," smiled Ron.

I took a load off and surveyed the courtyard. The light was just failing, and the party lights flicked on. I looked over my shoulder to see Mick, the owner of

Longboard's, standing by the light box, looking over the same scene as me. He was a short, powerfully built man of few words, but I could see the romantic in him as he gazed out at the pretty lights.

"You take care of that item for me?" I said. I had given Mick the gun I had taken from Brandon the Shark for efficient disposal. I don't like guns, and I especially don't like holding onto guns that might be linked to bad stuff—the kind that might cause a cop to come calling.

Mick grunted. "Yup."

"Never to be seen again?"

"Nup." He threw a tea towel over his shoulder and wandered away toward the kitchen without a further word. I sipped my beer and looked at Ron.

"Good day, Mr. Bennett?"

"Better than most. Breakfast on Lady Cassandra's balcony is always a fine start to any day."

"Indeed." I'd seen the balcony in question. It had the square footage of most two-bedroom apartments and happened to overlook the ocean on Palm Beach.

"And then I met with a prospective client at The Breakers."

"Good client?"

"Cashed up. The best kind. They paid for lunch, too. And you?"

"Spent the day with the Seminole."

I told Ron about my meeting with Jackie Bass, and Jimmy and Petal's view on things.

"I don't know, Ron. That casino is such a huge business. I find it hard to believe they're that concerned about jai alai."

"Well that reminds me," said Ron, nodding as Muriel placed another beer in front of him. "Guess what I heard at The Breakers?"

"Jackie Gleason's back and he's appearing there tonight?"

"That would draw a good crowd in Palm Beach, you're right. But, no. There's a private party this week being thrown by Elroy Hoskin."

"The Vegas guy?"

"That's the one. He owns half the strip, and now he's apparently rented a mansion on the island. The locals are calling it home base. Word is he's going to unveil a plan for a new Florida destination casino."

"In Palm Beach?" I said.

Ron shrugged. "No one knows."

"Man, I'd love to get into that party."

Ron sipped his beer and smiled. "Say the magic words."

"You didn't."

"The magic words?"

I shook my head. "Okay, the magic words: free beer."

"Ah, there you go. I spoke with the Lady Cassandra. She has procured invitations."

"She is worth her weight in—" I glanced at Muriel. She was shaking her head. Note to self: using weight as a means of comparing a woman to anything was bad. "She is one wonderful lady."

"Yes, she is," said Ron. "So dust off your tuxedo."

"Mine's always ready to go. Lenny would roll over in his grave if it were any other way."

We sipped on our beers, and Ron explained that Cassandra was at some charity committee meeting, so we ordered crunchy grouper sandwiches and shared a plate of smoked fish dip that Mick made himself from whatever fish came in on the boats. Today it was swordfish, and it was smoky awesomeness, paired with a nice cold beer. The bar started to fill up under the cover of darkness, and we were kicking back, watching absolutely nothing happen, when my cell phone buzzed in my pocket. I thought it might be Danielle, so I pulled it out.

"Hey," I said.

"*Hola?* Señor Miami?"

"This is he. Julio?"

Yes, señor, is Julio. I hope I do not disturb your evening."

"Not at all, Julio. What can I do for you?"

"I am sorry to call, but you remember Perez, one of the pelotari you met?"

I remembered meeting twelve handsome, athletic, roughly Spanish-looking guys. I remembered Perez was one of them. That was as good as it got.

"I remember. Why?"

"Señor Miami, somebody just tried to kill him."

CHAPTER SEVENTEEN

The Perez home was a nice two-story townhouse in Palm Beach Gardens. Well-tended lawns and clean, late-model cars. We parked short of the townhouse and walked in the sunshine to the front door. I stopped short to look at the front window. It had been boarded up with ply, and I stepped around the lawn in front to look at the footprints. There were about a hundred of them, so they told me nothing. I'd had a few beers in me when Julio called the previous night, and upon learning that the someone trying to kill Perez had actually been a brick thrown through his window, I told them to call the cops and that I'd be over first thing in the morning. I wished I had mentioned not trampling the lawn in fixing the window, but that was done.

The front door flew open, and I looked up to see Julio.

"Señor Miami," he said.

I nodded. "Hey, Julio." I looked around the small front yard, then wandered to the door.

"This is my colleague, Ron Bennett."

They shook hands, and Julio looked back to me.

"We did as you say last night, Señor Miami. The police came and took statements, and then we fix the window."

We stepped into the cool house, straight into a living room. The place was a newish build, maybe four or five years old. Below the smashed window a leather sofa and a couple armchairs stood sentry before a flat-screen television on the wall. Julio led us out to a small rear courtyard, where a woman and a man I now recognized as Perez sat at a patio table. Perez had a bandage wound around his head. He smiled and made to get up, but his wife told him to sit still. I went around and shook his hand, then that of his wife, and I introduced Ron.

"*Estás bien?*" I asked Perez.

He smiled. "*Sí, gracias.*"

Then I asked Perez to tell me what happened.

"His English is not so good. I will translate, okay?" said Julio.

Perez started talking and pointing at the inside of the townhouse, and Julio spoke to me.

"He says they were watching TV. He was lying on the sofa, the one under the window, when a brick—" Julio turned to Perez and spoke in Spanish, and Perez replied, then Julio continued. "It was, you call it, a cinder block."

I nodded.

"So the brick smashed the window and hit part of the arm of the sofa and part of his head." Julio pointed at the bandage, which I had picked up on all by myself. "He could have been killed, Señor Miami."

I didn't doubt that for a second. A cinder block would crush a human skull like a meat mallet on a hard-boiled egg. But I wasn't convinced they actually wanted to kill Perez. It was entirely plausible that the block hitting him had been an accident.

"Julio, you mentioned a note."

"Si," he said, directing us inside the house. He grabbed a cell phone off the kitchen counter and turned it on, then handed it to me. The small screen displayed a picture of a piece of paper that had been crumpled then flattened out.

"This was tied around the brick," said Julio.

The note read like Hemingway, direct and to the point.

JAI alAi dIEs OR You do.

The letters had been cut from a newspaper and stuck down. In this age of email and social media, I had forgotten such things were possible.

"The police took the note?"

Julio nodded.

"What did the police say?"

He shrugged. "They would try, but not to hope," he said.

It was lacking in bedside manner but was a fair assessment. Chances were the letters were from the local rag that was printed in the tens of thousands, and I guessed there were no fingerprints on the paper. Cinder block was the most popular building material in South Florida, so that wasn't going to narrow it down, either. I wandered back outside with Julio, and Ron went into the living room.

"Julio, tell Perez we'll keep looking, but the police are right. There really isn't much to go on."

Julio spat out a long line of Spanish, then nodded as Perez spoke back. Perez nodded at me.

"What?" I said.

"He forgot to mention his cousin."

"What about his cousin?"

"His cousin was coming to visit last night. He saw two men throw the brick."

I blinked my eyes hard. "He forgot that? Someone saw the guys, and he forgot that?"

Julio shrugged.

"Did his cousin get a description?"

"Si, he gave it to the policia," said Julio.

"Okay, that's good. That's something. So, Julio, can you tell me if his cousin got a good look at the men?"

Julio spoke in Spanish again, and Perez listened, looked at me, then spoke to Julio. Julio frowned at me.

"He says his cousin saw them good. He called at them, and they ran, but he saw them well enough."

"And what did they look like?" I asked.

"Tall men, long hair, tied back. No sleeves on their shirts. Headbands. Like the old movies."

"Like what old movies?"

Perez fired some more Spanish, and Julio looked at me.

"Cowboy movies," he said. "He said they looked like Indians."

CHAPTER EIGHTEEN

Ron played the nickel slots while I sat and half watched him and half watched the room, until I could bear it no more, and I went for a wander. Perez's cousin had said the two men were big guys, strong, with sleeveless shirts and tied back hair, like Indians. He said one had a circular tattoo on his arm but couldn't be more specific. So Ron and I decided to drive down to the Seminole casino and see if we found anyone fitting that description. It was like searching for a needle in a stack of needles. Everyone fit the description. The security, the croupiers, floor managers, bartenders, half the patrons. Pretty much every guy in the place fit the look in some way. Except for the tattoo. I walked around the gaming floor, then around past the stores and the hotel lobby, and then out around the pool. I was coming back into the building from the pool when a guy who fit the description just nicely stopped right in front of me. He was tall and muscular, broad arms under his suit jacket, and he had black hair, tied back. I couldn't tell about the tattoo.

"Mr. Jones," he said.

"Ah, yeah?"

"Mr. Bass would like to see you."

I got the distinct impression that when Jackie Bass wanted to see you, you got seen. So I found myself again in his large office overlooking the pool. The water looked plenty clean to me.

"Mr. Jones," said Bass, coming around his desk. His face was tight, not upset or angry, but not beaming the smile he had flashed so willingly the last time we met.

"Mr. Bass, what can I do for you?"

"Please, take a seat," he said.

I did. He did not.

"I'm wondering what it is I can do for you, Mr. Jones. A second visit? You are becoming quite the regular."

"It's a very nice casino you have here, Mr. Bass."

"I know it. But the thing is, I don't see you gambling, Mr. Jones. Trying out that comp gaming credit I offered you. What I see is you walking around our establishment, watching our employees. Watching our processes."

"Your processes?"

"Yes, sir. If I didn't know better I'd say you looked like you were casing our casino, planning some kind of heist." He said the last word through pursed lips, like saying the word would make it happen. "First you come here on some PR ruse, but I find out you are not in PR. You are a private detective."

I raised my eyebrow at the thought that he had been checking me out.

"Then you return, leaving your partner at the slots, and you walk around my casino, casing the smallest detail, looking for an employee that you might pull into your plan."

"That's pretty far-fetched, Mr. Bass."

"Is it, Mr. Jones? The video tells a pretty compelling story."

"What's your point, Mr. Bass?"

"My point is, I don't know what you are up to, but I suggest you take a vacation from this casino. Let me be clear. Don't come here. For your own good, Mr. Jones. I'm afraid if something were to go missing in the casino, your actions could make you look very guilty indeed."

I watched him now, and the smile never came. He was analyzing me, summing me up. I didn't know if his concern was real, but it was too close to the events with Perez for my liking.

"You know, Mr. Bass, I think you're right. I think I'll take a little break from casinos. After all, I'm really not a gambling man."

"A sound plan," said Bass, standing. He called for his guy, the big Seminole who had brought me up.

"Goodbye, Mr. Jones," said Bass, and the big guy and I headed out to the elevator. As we went down, I broke the silence.

"I'm thinking about getting a tattoo," I said. I looked at the big guy.

"What do you think? Would a tattoo look good on me? You have any tats?"

The big Seminole tilted his head slightly to look at me. He cocked one eyebrow, then turned his head back without uttering a word.

Sometimes things are worth a shot, even when they come to naught. And sometimes, they leave you stepping out of an elevator feeling like a fool. The guard walked me—not touching, but not more than an inch away—to the front door of the casino and deposited me there.

"Have a nice day," he said, and he spun and stepped back into the cave-like depths of the casino. Then the door flung open the other way, and Ron appeared.

"Saw you getting assisted out," he said. "Any problems?"

"Plenty. What are you referring to?"

"You getting kicked out of a casino?"

I nodded. "For not betting. That's got to be some kind of first, doesn't it?"

"Interesting timing," said Ron.

"My thoughts exactly. I just don't know what to do next."

"I do."

"What's that, Ron?"

"It's time to get your penguin suit on. We've got a party to go to."

CHAPTER NINETEEN

The Lady Cassandra walked up the steps of the
Tuscan-style mansion in a thin, blue-sequined dress that
split below the knee. It showed her to be in great shape
but showed no more. It was a classy look for a classy lady.
The diamonds in her ears glistened against blond hair that
held a hint of glamor despite being dulled by the years.
She had lost her husband in his prime, yet she was
naturally sanguine and up for an adventure—more so
than most people her age.

Ron beamed like a lottery winner, and perhaps that
was apt. He, too, looked toward life's brighter side, despite
his fair share of heartache, and his silver mane and the
glint in his eye made him the perfect companion for the
lady on his arm. Not to mention he looked great in a tux.

I hung back and let them walk together—never keen
to be a third wheel. Cassandra had procured four
invitations, but I'd had no stomach to find a date.

Danielle would have jumped at the chance to frolic with the jet set, and I consoled myself with the knowledge that she would have knocked so many socks off, we would have been the exact center of attention I wished to avoid. As it was, I lumbered up the steps to a white-clad waiter carrying champagne, and wondered what version of beer Danielle was getting into with her cop buddies in Atlanta. I checked my phone one last time, saw only her missed call to me and my missed return, and then I switched it to silent.

There was a lot of faux hugging and air-kissing going on. Dresses must not be crushed just because their wearers were happy to see each other. But Palm Beach wasn't that big a place, and throughout the winter I had no doubt these people repeated this effort numerous times, on each occasion greeting each other like long-lost friends. Ron and Cassandra dissolved into the crowd, as we had agreed. If they found or heard something of interest they'd find me. It wasn't that big a house. But it was plenty big. The entry hall alone was bigger than my house, including the lot it sat on. A long shallow pool led from the entrance to the open doors on the Intracoastal side, where the home opened up to a patio lit with tiki torches. I headed out to the patio to look at the lights, across to West Palm Beach. I really didn't think the view was any better than my place, and my house costs a hell of a lot less to keep cool. I was sipping my champagne when I felt someone brush up against my arm. I turned to find Jenny Almondson, the manager of West Palm Jai

Alai and Casino, looking at me. She had ditched the dark suit for a silver dress that appeared to have been painted on. Like Cassandra, Jenny's dress had a slit at the leg, but like the I-95, it went all the way to the border.

"Mr. Jones, I didn't expect to see you here." She gave me a smile like that wasn't a bad thing.

"Ms. Almondson. I didn't expect to be seen. Aren't you the competition?"

"It's Jenny. And the casino community isn't as big as you think, Mr. Jones. One might work for a certain casino today, but tomorrow, who knows?"

"Like baseball," I said.

"Perhaps. Just less . . . sweat." She nibbled her lip, then looked around the patio. I took a long slug of bubbles. I wasn't sure why she was laying it on so thick, but I hadn't reached the point where it had become any kind of hard work.

"Do you know our host, Mr. Hoskin?" I asked.

Jenny turned back to me. "Elroy Hoskin. Born 1950, Las Vegas, Nevada. Grew up around the strip. Sinatra, Deano, Sammy, he saw them all. He was managing his first casino one month after being of legal age and owned his first four years later. He now owns half the strip, plus that giant Ferris wheel, along with casino properties from the Caribbean to Macau."

I cocked an eye at Jenny. "You really a secret agent or something?" I said.

She smiled. It was a disarmingly hot smile. "I don't plan on managing jai alai for the rest of my life."

"At this rate, you'll be running a Vegas casino before the year is out."

She sipped some champagne.

"That's the plan."

CHAPTER TWENTY

We mingled with other guests, and I saw a few faces worth saying hello to, along with a few worth avoiding. I slipped back to the bar for refreshers and ran in to Eric Edwards. Upon seeing me he frowned, like he'd walked into the women's bathroom. He ran his hand down his chest, trying to smooth the necktie that wasn't there.

"What are you doing here?" he said.

"You're not the only one who's connected, you know."

"Ah, your mysterious Cassandra. I'm expecting an introduction."

"A promise is a promise," I said.

As I said it, I felt Jenny brush up against me, again with impeccably bad timing. "Aren't you going to introduce me?" she said.

Eric lifted an eyebrow and grinned. I could see his politician's mind clicking over. How can I use this to my advantage? It was still stuck in his craw that I had ended up with his ex-wife, and I had to admit I wasn't shy about lording it over him. It wasn't a classy look for me, but caring about Eric's feelings hadn't yet made it onto my bucket list. Eric would love nothing more than to drop it to Danielle that I was prancing about the island on the arm of a gorgeous blond while she was in Georgia. And then he went the other way.

"I'm Eric Edwards, state attorney," he said, extending his hand. "And Miami here is not known for his manners."

"Jenny Almondson," she said, as Eric took her hand and kissed it. He actually kissed it. I was there, I saw it.

"A pleasure, Miss Almondson."

"I'm sure," she smiled.

Eric turned to me, smiling like a child on Christmas morning. "So where is your lovely girlfriend, Danielle?" he said. The smugness on his face was visible, like he'd just wrecked my evening's plan.

"She's in Atlanta. At a conference."

"How convenient for you," he said.

"Not really. It means I don't have anyone to drive me home."

Jenny put her hand on my arm. "I'll make sure you get home," she said.

Gee, thanks.

"So I heard you're running for the state legislature, next time round," Jenny said to Eric, changing tack so hard the boom nearly hit me in the head.

Eric didn't miss a beat. "How do these stories get legs?" he said. "The party already has an incumbent in place."

"A bumbling old fool who thought the House Speaker was his mama," whispered Jenny.

Eric smiled. "Just a rumor, I assure you."

"Well, I for one think we need some new dynamic blood in Tallahassee."

Eric nodded his thanks.

"I'm just going to run to the little boys' room," I said, excusing myself from the Eric Edwards lovefest. I made a beeline for the main hall, where I found Ron and Cassandra chatting with the mayor of West Palm Beach.

"Having a good time, Miami?" asked Cassandra.

"Interesting, that's for sure. You?"

"It's impossible not to have a good time on Ron's arm," she smiled.

If I didn't know better, I would have said Ron blushed, but his face wore the pink ruddiness of years of sun and beers anyway, so it was hard to tell. Either way, it gave me a warm feeling to see them so happy.

"I think the show is about to begin," said Ron, as the lights dimmed across the property.

Fog began to cascade from the interior pool, and the far wall lit up with a scene of palm trees on a deserted beach. The low rumble of a string section permeated the air and grew in tension, dragging the stragglers from the patio into the house. There was no mistaking the Vegas in the presentation when a thunderclap pounded across the room, hitting me in the chest, more real than real, and the sound of rain washed over the gathering. A wind blew in from above, simulating a hurricane in the way only a guy from Nevada who had never seen more than a dust devil could present one. Ladies grabbed at their hair to prevent their expensive dos ending up as bedhead. Then, as suddenly as it began, it finished, and bird tweets replaced the wind. The soft glow of sunrise, approximated by a spotlight with yellow cellophane over it, rose over the beach scene. Then, through the magic of computer animation, a building rose from the beachfront, a stylized facade that looked like something from South Beach. Sort of art deco, but not. Some architect's vision of freshening the look. The building appeared, and the picture swept toward the building, over sleek cars and limos, right to the front door. Then we zoomed inside, like we were on a ride at one of the Orlando theme parks. Inside, the building looked clubby and dark, lots of wood and leather, along with attractive people with giant smiles and sensational orthodontic work. Then, the voiceover.

"Ladies and gentlemen, a new destination for the Palm Beaches. An elite-level, boutique resort for only the most discerning clientele. Welcome to the newest resort by Hoskin."

There was a break in the voiceover where I assumed we were supposed to clap, but that didn't happen. The music played underneath the audience's stony silence. Then the voice continued. It told us about the proposed facilities, the swimming pool, the air-conditioned tennis courts, the Broadway-quality entertainment. I'd been to Broadway, and I was entertained by a guy dressed as an M&M, so I wasn't that knocked out. The video showed attractive people, mostly of a certain age, having the time of their lives. I noted only one sweeping shot of a group of folks playing cards; otherwise there was no hint of gaming, especially not slot machines. The voiceover continued, and I wondered why Hoskin had bothered to rent the house when we could have watched the whole thing on the Internet in our pajamas.

"Hoskin Palm Beach will feature complimentary limousines to shuttle guests to the proposed main gaming and entertainment center in nearby West Palm Beach. In addition, those guests looking for more excitement can board our exclusive, high-speed catamaran that will take guests from Palm Beach to our proposed Miami resort in less than an hour, complete with complimentary champagne and gaming during the journey."

I looked around the room. There were a lot of frowns. I couldn't help but think Hoskin had misjudged his crowd. These people lived in Palm Beach because it wasn't Miami. They didn't want a shuttle bringing riff-raff to the island. And as for the most discerning clientele? In their not-so-humble opinions, the most discerning clientele already lived here. They didn't need to arrive in a free limo from West Palm.

The show finished in a big crescendo of strings and trumpets. I got ready for *Hail to the Chief* but it didn't happen. Instead, the voiceover introduced Elroy Hoskin.

Now there was a smattering of applause, for a real-life human being. Hoskin was shorter than I'd imagined him to be, and he looked younger than a guy who had met Sinatra. I wondered if he'd had any work done. He was stocky but looked in good shape, and his thick, brown curly hair covered his head like a helmet.

"Thank you, ladies and gentlemen, thank you. It has been my privilege to develop some of the world's most exclusive resort destinations: Vegas, Abu Dhabi, Macau, even Sydney, Australia. Now imagine the best of the best, for the best. That is Hoskin Palm Beach. I know what you are thinking. Crowds and traffic and neon lights. Well let me assure you, that is not Palm Beach, and it is not Hoskin Palm Beach. Our exclusive club will be a small community, just like the island itself. A place to relax, unwind, and enjoy the company of other discerning individuals."

Ron leaned into me. "When did discerning come to mean filthy rich?" he whispered.

I raised my eyebrows and watched the show.

"Imagine the best of everything you love about visiting New York or London or Paris, now at your fingertips right here at Hoskin Palm Beach. With our main proposed facility located in West Palm Beach, you will be a short limo ride from the full entertainment experience, but secluded from it as long as you remain on the Palm Beach resort."

A man in black stepped up to the stage and handed Hoskin a glass of champagne, and as he did, a fleet of trays sailed through the room, offering bubbles to everyone. Then Hoskin held his glass in the air.

"Ladies and gentlemen, I thank you for coming tonight, and I hope that you continue to enjoy yourselves. Let us toast. To Palm Beach."

It was a good point to end on. This crowd loved their island and would toast it with another man's bubbles at the drop of a hat. We toasted, then a smattering of applause saw Hoskin off the stage. The spotlight died, and the house lights came up just a touch, and lights appeared in the pool by our feet.

I turned to Ron, who was smiling and shaking his head, and Cassandra, who wore a pretty solid frown.

"Vegas on the beach," said Ron. "Awesome."

"I think not," said Cassandra. "A gambling house on the island? How ghastly."

"I thought the free ferry to Miami was a nice touch," I said.

"Where is this thing supposed to be, anyway?" said Cassandra.

"I heard they were taking over the Colonial Hotel property," said Ron.

"Oh, Ronnie, say that isn't so," said Cassandra.

The mayor of West Palm chipped in. "Word outside was Hoskin was going to buy the Everglades Club."

"Isn't Hoskin Jewish?" I said.

The mayor nodded.

"Hard to see them ever selling that place," said Ron. "Impossible to see them selling to a Jew."

The Everglades Club was an exclusive club that sat smack bang in the middle of the island on ritzy Worth Avenue. It was famous for having the most exclusive membership roster, one that reportedly managed by sheer accident to have no blacks, Jews, or women. Word was JFK's dad had resigned his membership back in the day, in protest over their restrictive membership policies.

"Well I don't care for that club, and I don't care for Hoskins Palm Beach. Plain old regular Palm Beach is fine with me," said Cassandra.

I was tempted to mention that there was nothing regular about Palm Beach but thought better of it. I turned instead to the mayor.

"So, Your Honor. I've heard about this major entertainment center in West Palm. You keeping it for a surprise?" It wouldn't be the first time in Florida that politicians had forgotten to mention a major development until after it was too late. But the mayor shook his head.

"News to me, old boy. I'm sure we'll assess any application on its merits, but there is a distinct distaste among the electorate for more gambling. Besides, the Compact is being renegotiated, and I would be surprised if Tallahassee turns its back on all that money."

As he finished, Elroy Hoskin appeared at his shoulder, doing the glad-handing bit of the show. He had good help with an assistant at his shoulder, letting him know who everyone was. It was good work, and made Hoskin look like he gave a damn about every individual.

"Mr. Mayor, so happy you could join us," said Hoskin, going for the two-handed pump.

"Pleasure is mine, sir. Quite the show. I'd be interested in hearing more about this West Palm Beach property."

Hoskin smiled. "Early days, of course. We have a few matters to overcome with the state, don't we? But I think all the jobs and tourism dollars we can bring to the city of West Palm Beach will help them see it from the right point of view, don't you agree?"

"Perhaps," said the mayor.

"I'd love to chat about it over lunch," he smiled. "I'll have my people call you."

Hoskin moved onto Cassandra, who again he knew by name, and then Ron, who he did not. Then he turned to me.

"And Miami Jones, a pleasure," he said.

I shook his hand and checked his ear for one of those little earbuds that spies use, but found nothing.

"I like the look of your high-speed ferry," I said.

"Don't you? I love those things. We run one between Hong Kong and Macau. Really something. Did you know they are made in Tasmania, Australia?"

"I did not."

"It's true. Ours will be the fastest ever."

I believed it.

Hoskin nodded to us all and moved on, assistant at his shoulder, smiling for the next group of well-heeled freeloaders. On that note I decided to get more champagne. I offered to do a run.

"How are you getting home, Miami?" said Cassandra.

"Ferry?" I said.

"I have a spare room. You are staying with me. Now, I for one will have some more of that awful man's champagne," she smiled, winking at me.

I liked her a lot. Not just because she made Ron so happy, but because she was stinking rich, and she didn't deny she enjoyed what wealth offered her, yet she still didn't believe her own press. She knew it was, like many things in life, just dumb luck.

We all decided to make a bar run outside to see the lights of West Palm across the water. The marina was lit up, and we could hear music coming from a bar on the esplanade. I got four flutes and passed them to Ron, Cassandra and the mayor. The mayor was one of those guys who believed in his city and its people and who wanted to make the place he lived better for everyone. He was never going to rise from local politics. His suits were baggy and his comb-over not television friendly. He had lost his wife to cancer during his last campaign and had garnered a fair sympathy vote. But I gave him kudos for not wearing it on his sleeve.

"What do you think, Your Honor? Jobs, money into the economy. Sound like a good deal?" I said.

The mayors of Palm Beach and West Palm Beach looked after cities separated by a sliver of water, but might as well have been on different worlds. Palm Beach had been founded by Henry Flagler, the owner of Standard Oil. His name was ubiquitous in Florida, as it seemed every second thing was named after him. He had built the railway from St. Augustine in the north, to Miami in the south, and in doing so had bought up all the property where he planned to build stops for the train. On that land, he had built lavish hotels. His personal favorite was Palm Beach. It became a winter retreat of choice for the New York elite to escape the snow. But although the hotel was on the island, the train stop was across the Intracoastal Waterway on the mainland. As happens, businesses popped up around the train station, serving not only the needs of the wealthy guests in Palm Beach, but eventually providing housing to the service staff who worked on the island. The city of West Palm Beach was born. Now it dwarfed the town it was created to serve and had all the issues of every American city. The kinds of issues that didn't affect the wealthy residents of Palm Beach. Issues like jobs and pumping money into the cash registers of local businesses.

The mayor shrugged. "It sounds good, but I'm not sure, Miami," he said. "I've seen it happen, spoken with other mayors around the country. Big new development promises jobs, money. But that only works if the jobs are new, if people who aren't working can get work, or if it brings new people to the area. But our research says that most of the jobs a casino would create are actually jobs that already exist in the city. You have a big new casino that employs thousands, but what about the stores, restaurants, bars that the casino puts out of business? The net gain of jobs is close to zero, and the money just moves from local business people to some huge conglomerate."

"Sounds awful," said Cassandra.

"That's just one point of view," said the mayor. "Sometimes there are new jobs. That's why we have to evaluate each proposal. But lights and smoke and fancy videos don't sway me. There's too much at stake."

I put my hand on his shoulder. "I wish there were more men like you in Tallahassee, Your Honor."

He smiled sheepishly, for we both knew it would never happen.

"Speaking of Tallahassee," I said, as Eric approached with Jenny.

As promised, I introduced Eric to Cassandra, and Jenny to everyone. Eric charmed the group, and Jenny looked the part on his arm. For a second I felt jealous. And then I didn't.

I just felt sad, and I couldn't pin down why.

CHAPTER TWENTY—ONE

I moved away from Eric holding court and wandered around the house. In my experience, anything worth happening at a party is probably happening upstairs. It was a truism in college, and it was just as true now. I climbed the staircase and found a massive foyer at the top that looked down on the reflection pool. The foyer opened out onto a balcony. I stood looking out past the balcony, when a door near me opened. Elroy Hoskin stepped out, carrying a small wooden box.

"Mr. Jones, just the man. Would you join us for cigars?"

I sat on a wicker chair that was topped by the most comfortable cushion I had ever sat on. This thing was like putting your cheeks onto a cloud. Hoskin passed cigars around to the small group. The collective wealth of the gathering was in the billions. But that's the thing about a tuxedo. It's a great leveler. Everyone looks like a billionaire in a tux. My friend and mentor Lenny Cox always said that there wasn't a room you couldn't get into in Palm Beach if you were wearing a tuxedo. Seemed it applied to private balconies, as well.

"So, Mr. Jones," said Hoskin, lighting his cigar, the end glowing with ash. "You are a transplant to these parts. How would you read the mood of the room tonight?"

I clipped the end off my cigar and waited for the lighter to come around.

"You mean after your presentation? Skeptical, I'd say."

Hoskin nodded. "If you had to rate our chances of getting this project off the ground, gut feeling, what would you say?"

"Out of ten? A solid two." I took the lighter off the gray haired gent next to me and puffed the cigar.

Hoskin smiled. "You don't sugar-coat it, do you Jones? I like that." He turned to the other men in the group. "Yes-men are easy to find. The other kind, not so much."

The group all nodded as one, and looked at me like I was about to be the subject of a bidding war for my business consulting services.

"If you were on this project, what would you do?" Hoskin said to me.

I shook my head. "Not really my area."

"I hear you are quite perceptive, and, I see, not afraid to voice an opinion. I'm not looking for an MBA analysis;

I have those by the truckload. I'm looking for street smart. Your gut."

I didn't know if the guy was buttering me up or not, but the cigar was a real Cuban, and a butler-looking dude had just arrived with a decanter of brandy, so I played along.

"If I were on the project? I'd be looking for somewhere else to do it."

Hoskin raised his eyebrow. "You don't strike me as the quitting type."

"Not quitting. But when the cards are stacked against you, sometimes it pays to play another table."

Hoskins nodded and sniffed his brandy. "I like that metaphor. Do you mind if I use it?"

"All yours."

"But really, you'd cut and run?"

"The State is in a bind with the Compact, the people here don't like the idea of anyone from outside spoiling their paradise, and the small size of your project makes me wonder how the numbers trump the effort."

"Nice evaluation. But I didn't become a success by giving up."

"I'm not suggesting giving up. Rather, having a plan B," I said.

Hoskins focused on me, like an exhibit in a museum. "You almost made it to the major league, is that right?"

"You have good intel, sir. Yes, I got onto the Oakland pitching roster."

"But you didn't play."

"No, I never got to play."

He watched me, looking for that sorrow in the eye that thoughts of glory days bring. But he wasn't going to find it. I didn't get all misty eyed over my baseball career. I'd played, done my best, and moved on. I'd be lying if I said it hadn't twisted in my gut at the time, getting to the majors but then never getting the chance to even throw one pitch in anger. But I had reconciled it, long ago. I'd had my chances. I went further than most but not as far as some. Some men would be ruined by making it within a hundred feet of the Everest summit, only to never see the top. I was okay with having gotten to see the view at all.

"You played a couple of years down here in Florida, then you quit."

"I don't see it like that."

"Quitters never do."

I smiled. "Are you trying to bait me, Mr. Hoskin?"

He leaned back in his chair and puffed his cigar. Then he smiled. "Not at all. I just like to know the measure of a man."

"Let me ask you a question," I said. "Did you play baseball as a kid? Throw it in your yard with your dad?"

"Of course, I was an American boy." He smiled at the group.

"But you didn't play professionally. Did you quit?"

"I see what you're trying to do, but no. I didn't quit. I took other opportunities."

"My point exactly."

Hoskin nodded and put his cigar down and leaned toward me. "You have your ear to the ground here. I've spoken to people, and your name keeps coming up. So I'd like to make you an offer. Keep your ear to the ground for me. You hear anything at all, you let me know. I will build my resort in Florida. I can outwait the politicians; I can outwait the damned Indians. You do this for me, I'll make it worth your while."

He nodded and pulled a silver case from his pocket and took out a business card.

"My personal number. Anything you think is worth knowing over the next few days, I want to know. If things aren't going my way, I want to know ASAP, so I can act. Now if you'll excuse us, we do have some boring business to discuss."

I took the card and bid the group a good evening. I wandered back downstairs where music was now playing, and I saw Ron and Cassandra dancing. I didn't see Eric or Jenny, and I didn't want to. I sent Ron a text saying I'd see myself home, and I turned and walked out the front door. A fleet of town cars were shuttling guests all over the island, so I got one to Cassandra's apartment, then collected my car and headed home. I went into the empty bedroom to kick off my shoes and undo my tie. The black tie hung around my neck, and I undid a button on my shirt. As I turned from the room, I caught my reflection in the mirror. I looked myself over. For a guy my age I was in good shape, although the muffin top had crept in over the past months. I had been running less, and happiness had started to turn to flab. I told myself it was just age catching up with me. Then I caught myself, my thinking. I was prefacing every thought with *for a guy my age*. I looked at the sandy blond hair, at the lines on my face. It wasn't the face of a boy on the edge of something great. It was a man's face, weathered by experience. And, despite my protestations to the contrary, tinged with regret. Just like Sinatra, I had too few to mention, but they were there.

I stood there in my tux, not looking as good as I ever did, but as good as I ever would. For a moment, I wanted to go back. To spring afternoons, throwing pitch after pitch in the cages, until the dark came and my mother called. I wanted to go back and quit practice early, so I could spend more time with my mother before she was taken from me. I wanted to reconsider my choice of college, to not leave Connecticut for Florida, so I could drive my grieving father from the bar and save the lives of him and the student he hit. I wanted to go back and move faster, step in front of the bullet that took Lenny Cox, the man who taught me everything worth knowing.

I wandered out into the living room and grabbed the scotch bottle and a glass and slid out to the patio. I poured a long glass and looked at the empty lounger beside me. I smiled. *How pitiful we are, Miami Jones. How pitiful indeed.* I took a long drink and lay back on my lounger, looking at the dark water before me, and I thought of my college pitching coach. He told me I would get hit. For bases, for runs, for homers. He said some of my pitches would get hit so far they would never find the ball. But once done, it was done. The guys who sweated the last one, let the thought that they should have thrown the curve rather than the heat rattle around their brain, those guys got hit again and again. Those guys didn't make it. Because they lived in the past, and a good batter was very much the present. Forget the last one, he told me. Focus on the next one. It's the next one that might be the one that defines you.

CHAPTER TWENTY–TWO

I was nursing a minor hangover in my office when my office manager, Lizzy put the call through. Good fortune had bestowed itself upon me, and I had fallen asleep on my patio after the second Scotch, so I sipped water and halfheartedly looked over paperwork while thinking through events from the previous evening. I seemed to have been put on the payroll of a major Vegas casino in some way, shape or form, although I certainly hadn't accepted the nebulous position. When the phone beeped I hoped it was Danielle, having missed her call again while enjoying Cubans with Elroy Hoskin, but it wasn't.

"He says his name is Roto," said Lizzy. "I can't decipher any more than that."

"Thanks, Lizzy." I hit the button on the phone. "Roto?"

"Señor Miami?"

"Yes, Roto," I smiled. I couldn't get over the whole thing with the single names, though I was disappointed not to have met a Ronaldo. Then I dropped the smile as I remembered these guys never called me with good news.

"Is everything all right?"

"It's Julio."

"What about him?" I said, standing.

"He just got fired."

I was hungry by the time I reached the fronton, and I hoped it wouldn't dictate my mood. Julio was sitting in his car, parked on the street across from the casino, having been escorted from the premises by security.

"What happened?" I said through the window.

Julio got out and waved his hands like a madman. "They fired me, señor. I arrived for practice, I get called to manager's office, and lady manager fires me."

"Why, Julio? Did they give you a reason?"

"Si, they said I was fixing jai alai, making bets."

"And that's not true?"

His face sank, like my lack of support cut him to the bone. "No, señor. It is not true. It is never true. I am set up."

I wandered into the fronton. A performance was underway and two pelotari tossed the ball at the wall with the energy of someone finishing a swim across the English Channel. They had a job to do, and they didn't want to get fired themselves, so the show went on, sans enthusiasm. Roto was on the bench of players rotated out, and he came to me.

"What happened, Roto?"

"Is a set-up, Señor Miami. Because Julio did not stop promoting the jai alai."

"Let me ask you something, Roto, and forgive me. Could Julio do this?"

He shook his head so hard it moved inside his scratched-up helmet. "No, señor. Is not possible."

"I know you are friends, Roto, but this is important."

"No, señor. You misunderstand. I do not think Julio would do this thing, but what I say to you is, he could not do it."

"Why couldn't he?"

Roto glanced back to check the play. His turn would be a while coming, as the pair on court were throwing daisies for each other in a form of protest.

"People think because there is so much betting on jai alai, that it must be crooked. But this is not true. Look at the court." He pointed toward the play. "Two men play. When one man wins, he gets a point. The other man leaves the court. The next player on the bench comes on court. They play once more, and the winner of this point stays, the loser goes, and this keeps rotating around until one player gets to a total of seven points. He is the winner."

"Okay, so?"

"So to fix the game, you would need to have at least four men involved in the fix, maybe more. Less than this, the others could easily upset the fix."

"All right, I can see that. But the casino is just going to say there were more of you involved."

He shook his head. "But they did not, señor. You do not close your investigation and fire one player if there are others who may be crooked. Is not sensible."

He made a good point. It looked like Julio had been targeted. By whom and why I couldn't say.

What I could say was that I wasn't going to be able to bluff my way up to the executive floor this time. The blank slate of a security guard I'd conned the first time I visited Jenny Almondson was gone, replaced by a thick-bodied, stern-looking Polynesian. Through a face devoid of emotion, he looked down on me, which put him at around six five, and I couldn't get within three feet of him, which put him at about four hundred pounds. I could hear the breath coming through his nose.

"Ms. Almondson," I said with a nod.

For a moment he was motionless, as if he hadn't heard. Then his eyelids dropped as if to say, not today.

"It's about Julio," I said. Nothing. "Okay, tell her Miami Jones is here. I'll be waiting in the bar."

I ordered an OJ, but it didn't get to me. Before the bartender could even take the carton from the fridge, I heard my name from the door. I turned to see the big islander standing there. He mopped his brow with a kerchief, as if the effort of crossing the gaming floor had taken its toll.

"She'll see you," he puffed.

I turned to look at the bartender, and he waved me on. I started to follow the big guy back to the elevator, but it was a tedious journey, so I broke ranks and marched ahead. I didn't bother with the elevator, hitting the stairs, and came out onto the second floor where I found another Polynesian waiting for me. This one was a little older and about half the size of the guy downstairs. But he was no less intimidating. He wore a dark suit with no tie, shirt open at the neck, and his muscular frame filled every inch of it. He had tattoos up his neck and onto the side of his dark face and an explosion of hair out the back.

"Mr. Jones," he said. "This way."

He led me through the reception area back to Almondson's office. Jenny had morphed again, from the glamorous look of the previous evening back to buttoned-up and all business. Sort of. She smiled from behind her desk, phone to her ear, and I had to let out a breath. She'd make a burlap sack look good. I waited on the wing of the big Polynesian until Jenny hung up the phone, then she waved me forward. She met me on my side of the desk and kissed my cheek and gave me a quick, semi-professional hug, although I really wasn't sure how hugs fitted into an office situation.

"How are you, Miami?" she asked, and I wondered for a moment whether she could possibly have forgotten why I was there. It wasn't a social call.

"I missed you last night," she said, offering me a chair and leaning on the desk in front of me.

The Polynesian stood beside me. I might have been reading too much into it, but I felt boxed in.

"I looked for you," Jenny continued.

"Had to see a man about a dog," I said. I nodded at the big guy. "Who's your friend?"

"This is Mr. Finau. He's our head of security."

Finau nodded, but stayed silent.

"One of yours, downstairs?" I said.

Finau nodded again. He was a man of many words.

"I took your advice," said Jenny. "Beefed up security, starting with the personnel. Mr. Finau has brought in some of his people, who I think will do the job. What do you think, Miami?"

"Your man downstairs certainly fits the part."

"I've put extra security on the fronton, too, just so you know," said Jenny.

"Speaking of which," I said.

Jenny pursed her lips.

"Julio," she said.

"What gives?"

"He was fixing games, Miami. I know you understand the pressure we are under to comply with gaming regulations. We can't have even the scent of impropriety."

Something smelled, all right, but it wasn't impropriety.

"It looks pretty suspicious," I said. "First he's threatened, then days later he loses his job for allegedly fixing the game he was threatened for promoting."

"But fix it he did. I'm not happy about this, Miami. I told you, I like the guys. But when I'm presented with proof, I am required to act, regardless of whether I like the guys or not."

I leaned back in my chair.

"What proof?" I said.

Jenny leaned her head to one side and her golden hair fell away from her ear. Today she wore no earrings. "I'm afraid I can't get into that with you," she said.

I frowned, giving her the full wrinkled glory. "You can't or won't?"

"Can't, so I won't. This is not just answering a few questions. There are privacy issues."

"You're stonewalling me, Jenny. What gives?"

"I'm doing no such thing," she said, calmly. "You are asking for information that I can only release to Julio or his appointed attorney. And you are neither."

"So that's how you're going to play it?"

"Miami, that's how I have to play it. Think about it. You could be anybody. I've never actually had any communication from any of the pelotari that you represent them in any way. Now I'm not saying you don't. I'm just saying that legally, I can't tell you any more than this. Our security team led by Mr. Finau here," she said, nodding at the big silent unit, "conducted an investigation as required by gaming regulations. Mr. Finau found evidence that Diego Alvarez, or Julio as he is called, has been involved in the fixing of jai alai games. And before you say anything Miami, yes the evidence is compelling enough for me to dismiss him. I assure you I did not take that decision lightly."

I looked up at her and then at Finau. Jenny looked genuinely upset by events, as if she had made the tough decision required of her position, but that didn't mean she was happy about it. Finau on the other hand, gave me a look like he was totally focused on his breathing. It was a face that reminded me of the quiet summer afternoons I grew up with in New England. The ones that could turn ugly in an instant, depending on the direction of the wind. I decided there was nothing more for me there, so I shrugged and stood.

Jenny bumped off the desk and put her hand on my arm. "I'm sorry, Miami. Maybe you didn't know Julio like you thought you did. Maybe none of us did."

I nodded and moved away.

"Mr. Finau will show you out."

"Don't bother," I said. "I know the way."

I did know the way, but that didn't stop Finau from shadowing me to the front door. I didn't ask him any questions, because I knew I would be wasting my breath, and he didn't offer so much as a grunt. I stepped out into the glorious sunshine, which didn't suit my mood at all.

Jenny was right. Maybe I didn't know Julio like I hoped I did. But I did know one thing. When only one side is willing to talk, they are usually the custodians of the truth. And the other side probably has something very interesting to tell. If you can get it out of them.

CHAPTER TWENTY—THREE

I was tired, hungry and irritable by the time I left the casino, and I almost sideswiped a black pickup that cut across me into the parking lot, obviously in a hurry to drop some cash at the poker tables. I cursed the other driver, not even remotely interested in who might actually have been at fault, and I drove like a maniac back to Longboard's. The place was quiet and no one was behind the bar. I took a stool and cursed the lack of service. Then Mick wandered out from the darkness of the inner bar, towel draped across his tank top-clad shoulders. I had half an idea to give him a piece of my mind, but fortunately the better half prevailed. Being a bartender, or even a bar owner like Mick, one must pick up a sixth sense for people, their moods, their wants. Without asking, Mick poured me an iced tea from a pitcher and dropped it down in front of me.

"We got fresh Mahi. Sandwich. Coleslaw," he said, not so much delivering the daily specials as ordering for me.

He nodded to himself and walked away toward the kitchen, and I sipped some iced tea, then dropped my forehead to the wooden bar. There was some kind of cleaning solution residue on it, and it burned my nose, but I stayed there, eyes closed, until the plate hit the bar beside me. Mick nodded and leaned back against the inside bar taps and watched me. I lifted my head to find a delicious-looking fish sandwich before me. It was simple, like Mick. Lightly toasted hoagie roll, wood-grilled Mahi, tartar sauce, tomato, Vidalia onion, a leaf of romaine. It was sensational, smoky from the wood fire, and I felt all the better for it.

"Thanks, Mick," I said. "Just what the doctor ordered."

Mick nodded. "Yep."

Refreshed by a good meal and some sparkling conversation, I headed back to my office. I cruised by the monolithic county court building, casting its vast shadow over the parking lot into which I pulled. The lot sat between the court buildings and the new-construction office block that housed a multitude of small businesses, including one Lenny Cox Investigations. Lenny had left the business to me in his will, and since we already had the letterhead, I never changed the name.

The hybrid engine of the Escape kicked in, and the car fell silent as I backed into a space in the lot. I was slipping out of my seat belt when a big black truck skidded to a stop in front of my parking space. I couldn't be burden-of-proof sure, but I was confident it was the same pickup that had cut me off in the Jai Alai and Casino parking lot. For a moment I was happy about that, ready to give them some verbal for their earlier indiscretion. But then my brain played catch-up, and I realized how suspicious it was that the same truck was in front of me now. I held off opening the door and left the key in the ignition, hand on the gear selector. The black truck had tinted windows, so I couldn't see who was inside, but they weren't in any hurry. The truck joggled some from the engine revs, clearly in need of a tune-up. Then the door opened, and I watched a large, pale, bald guy climb out gingerly. It was the guy from the fronton who had taken Desi's money. He stepped one leg to the ground, then edged himself down, grimacing. He looked like a man with busted ribs. I saw his buddy, Redhead, come around the back of the truck, holding a handgun. It looked boxy and modern, squarish in shape, which made me think it was a Glock. That thought didn't fill me with joy. I don't like guns in the same way I don't like cancer, or any other thing whose sole purpose is to kill me. But I particularly don't like modern handguns with magazines. That's pretty much triple the number of bullets of a six-shooter, which affected the odds against me dramatically. There was a car parked behind me, and the Boston boys' truck was in front, so I wasn't about to go anywhere in the Escape. Which made me curse the name of the SUV. You'd think if you drove such a car, it would at least do what it said on the rear liftgate and help me escape. No such luck. Baldy took position in front of the car, his maneuverability clearly affected by the kicking in the ribs. Redhead pointed the gun at me through the windshield. The courthouse threw a shadow across him, but even then I could see the two black eyes that Lucas had given him. His face was puffy, like a bad boxer.

It wasn't the first time someone had tried to kill me. It wasn't even the first time it had happened in this very parking lot, and I briefly wondered what the value was in being between the massive courthouse, the offices of the state attorney, and the local police station, if it was such a great spot to beat on someone. The thought didn't linger though, because Redhead spoke.

"We lost our jobs because of you, you maggot!" He stood at the front corner of the car, driver's side, gun at my head. I didn't like where he was. The thing about guns is this: you have a chance if they are too far away to be accurate, or too close that you can disarm the shooter. But this guy was at just the right distance, where I couldn't touch him, but he wasn't going to miss, at least hitting the windshield. I put my foot on the brake and edged the selector into drive, and left my other hand on the door release. I couldn't outrun a bullet, but I wasn't going to sit there and take one, either. I edged my finger onto the window button and the electric motor pulled it down.

"Stop mumbling," I said. "I can't understand a word you say."

"You're a dead man!" screamed Redhead.

"What? You got sinus problems? Is your nose full of blood? I can't understand your stupid Red Sox accent."

I saw the guy grimace and that it hurt. His head shuddered, like he was on a rollercoaster, and the gun wavered. He was mad, that much I could say. Generally I have a life rule that is the equivalent of don't poke the bear. I broke that rule a lot. Here I was antagonizing a man who had a gun and very much wanted me dead. But to paraphrase Sherlock Holmes, if you eliminate all the sensible options, the last choice left, however ridiculous, is the one you have to run with.

Baldy said something I didn't hear but looked, from my average lip-reading to be *get him*, and Redhead began snaking toward me. He moved along the front fender until he reached where the tire was. At that point he had a choice to make: keep aiming at me through the windshield, or move past the windshield pillar and aim through the open window. I leaned back in my seat as much as possible, pressing my head against the headrest, to help him make his choice. Then he chose. And he chose poorly.

As the gun and his eyes moved by the steel frame of the windshield, I knew his vision would momentarily refocus on the car, away from me. So I moved. At the same time, I lifted my foot from the brake and punched the accelerator, wrenching the door open with as much force as I could muster. The hybrid electric engine might have been quiet, but it lacked power, so things took an uncomfortable second to kick in. Then the vehicle

lurched forward, crushing Baldy between it and the truck.
He bellowed a scream as his femur and knees were
smashed, and he was pinned, flopping forward onto the
hood of the Escape. The door shot into Redhead, which
would not have been a huge impact except for the
movement of the car, which drove the steel panel into his
midriff and knees. Despite what crash-test dummies
would have us believe, cars don't have a lot of give in
them. Getting hit by a door at even five miles per hour is
like a decent punch. Redhead buckled over and his upper
body lurched through the open window. He tried to aim
at the driver's seat, but he was too slow, and I wasn't there
anymore. As the SUV hit the truck, I dove out the door. I
now had a big metal barrier between the gun and me, so I
scrambled on hands and knees along the side of the
Escape, then behind the car parked beside it. I got to my
feet and ran across the next row, dropping behind a
sporty-looking Ferrari—no doubt the ride for someone
making an appearance in the court across the road. I
figured the Ferrari would give me the most time. Redhead
was going to recover, and he would either set out after me
or move my SUV to release his buddy. I wasn't sure
which, since I didn't know the nature of their
relationship. But either way, I figured when he came
looking, he would go for the trucks first. They provided
the biggest hiding spots, and drew the eye. No one in
their right mind would hide behind a little sports car in a
lot full of pickups. At least, that's what I hoped he would
think.

In any event, either their relationship was strong or the wailing was too much, because Redhead pulled my SUV back to let Baldy drop to the ground. As he did that, I pulled out my cell phone and made a call.

"Office of the State Attorney," said a voice I didn't know, but bet all the palm trees in the city belonged to a cute paralegal.

"This is Miami Jones. Tell Edwards there are armed men shooting up the parking lot right under his window."

I hung up. I didn't want to chat, and if I needed to explain, then I was done for anyway. But I knew Eric, or at least I thought I did. He was one of those state attorneys, the kind with higher political aspirations, whose popularity rose and fell with the crime rate. And one thing a crime-fighting state attorney doesn't want is gunplay in the parking lot outside his building. I dropped to my belly and looked across the asphalt. There was close to no clearance under the Ferrari, which added to its attraction as a hiding spot, but made it hard to see the feet of the thug coming to get me. I was pretty confident Baldy wasn't going anywhere. But as I watched, I saw boots that I assumed belonged to Redhead edging past a car in the row between us. The boots got to the row at the front of the Ferrari and moved along toward a line of trucks. When I'm right, I'm right. I crept like a lizard along the side of the Ferrari, keeping the stallion between me and that gun. Redhead's boots jumped to the back of the row of trucks, surprise, then spun around the other way. Finding nothing, he started moving back in my

direction. He was two pickups away from me when I
heard the footsteps. Running. Multiple hard-soled shoes
on pavement. I heard the footsteps break ranks and head
in at least two directions. Then I heard them slow,
showing caution. No one with a brain runs full speed into
gunplay, even the brave ones. Turning up at all was brave
enough. I figured it was time for all or nothing.

I stuck my head out the back of the Ferrari.

"Hey, go Yankees!" I whispered, just loud enough for
Redhead to hear. There's nothing a son of New England
despises more than the New York Yankees, so I saw the
red mist rise, and I ducked back behind the Ferrari as he
lifted the gun toward me. He popped off two shots, both
of which hit the asphalt nearby, and I revised my earlier
thought about how close he would have to get to hit me.
This guy was no sharpshooter. At the sound of gunfire a
chorus of voices called out to freeze, put the gun down,
police! Perhaps Redhead was disoriented, perhaps he was
just plain stupid, but his choice was to turn and fire a
volley of shots in the direction of the voices. He didn't
empty the gun, he just stopped firing, and then I heard a
volley of shots coming the other way. Unlike Redhead,
these shots came from guys who were trained, and I
heard several bullets make contact and the sound of a
body hitting the deck. There were more footsteps, then
more shouting, this time from over near my SUV. I
figured Baldy was already in the position the police
wanted him. Several sets of footsteps stopped near
Redhead. Then, after a moment of silence, I heard a call.

"Miami Jones," said the voice.

"Don't shoot," I replied. I crawled out from beside the Ferrari, my hands well away from my body. There were three cops crouched around the prone frame of Redhead. He looked paler than usual, which wasn't a good sign. Not for him, anyway.

"How many of them?" asked the cop nearest me.

"Just the two."

The cop spoke into a handset attached to his shoulder. "You have one suspect?" he said.

"One, sir," crackled the response.

"We have one as well. All suspects accounted for. All clear," he said. The three cops stood.

"You packing, Jones?" asked the cop.

"No. I'm not armed."

He nodded. "Get up, you look ridiculous."

I stood and brushed myself off. I didn't go over to the cops. I didn't really want to see Redhead. He was dead because of his own stupidity, or his own choices, or at least the choices he'd been able to make given his frame of reference. It was a deep philosophical hole I was staring into, so I turned away and looked across to my Escape. I could hear the whimpering coming from Baldy, and I saw the cops all standing over him. They weren't offering assistance, but then I figured they didn't carry ibuprofen on them.

Before long some paramedics arrived and got Baldy on a gurney, and he left handcuffed inside an ambulance. I was told to wait, which I did. I lifted the tailgate on the

Escape and sat down. A medical examiner's van rolled up and some photos were taken, and tape run around, then the body was removed. After the mess had been tidied up, I saw the lanky frame of Eric Edwards wander across the lot from his office. He smoothed his tie as he walked.

"Friends of yours, Jones?" he said, as he approached me.

"Hardly." I wasn't in the mood to even try to think of a witty retort. I didn't like Redhead, and he had tried to kill me, but regardless, a dead body had just been driven away and it left me deflated. It wasn't the first death I'd seen and probably wouldn't be the last unless I got my PGA ticket and starting teaching golf, but it wasn't something I ever planned on getting comfortable with.

"Tell me," said Eric.

So I told him. About the illegal betting and how I had upset the applecart. I told him Jenny Almondson had beefed up security, but I didn't tell him that it really had nothing to do with the betting. I told him I had driven some business away, and Baldy and Redhead had come for retribution. I left Desi out of the story, as well as Lucas.

"So it looks like I saved your bacon again," said Eric.

"Again? I don't recall the first time. And I'd say this time I did you a favor. Imagine what my dead body outside your window would do for your business."

"Imagine what it would have done for yours," he said.

Touché.

"What are you getting at, Eric?"

"You had cigars with Elroy Hoskin at the party."

"Are you sore because you got left out?"

"I'd like to meet him," said Eric.

I nodded. I got it. Good to have donors on all sides.

"Lady Cassandra not enough for you?" I said.

"Lady Cassandra is delightful and will be a wonderful supporter. But that was then. What have you done for me lately?"

"You're a piece of work, Eric, I tell you. Fine, next time I see Hoskin, I'll mention you. Make an introduction."

"Good," he said, smoothing his tie again. We heard the sound of squeaky brakes and turned to see a news van arrive outside the parking lot.

Eric gave his tie an extra patting down, then smiled. "Excuse me. I have to tell the good people of the Palm Beaches we have taken out some more bad guys."

I was pretty sure his *we* did not include me, so I watched him stride over to the news crew, then I told the cop in charge of the scene that I was going to my office, and if he wanted a statement he knew where to find me. He told me to wait, that he'd be done with me when he said so. I turned away and wandered across the lot. The news crew was setting up a camera and lights, and a pretty blond reporter was chatting to Eric. I left the cops to their stuff, I left my car open with the keys inside, and I headed over to my office, both for some reflection time and some hard liquor.

CHAPTER TWENTY—FOUR

I didn't go to my office, not right away. As I reached the front door I noted the nameplates of my fellow tenants, and one name stuck out, firing my synapses off in all sorts of directions and giving me an idea. I dropped into the offices of Croswitz and Allen, Attorneys at Law. They were the sort of law firm that one often found in the orbit around courthouses, surrounded by bail bondsmen and check cashing outlets. The sort of law firm that specialized in taking the low-hanging fruit, and shied away from anything too big, or too legally taxing. The partners in the firm were the firm, except that Allen had retired to Naples a few years earlier. He'd established a mailbox in a packing store over on the Gulf Coast, which enabled the firm to claim offices in both cities, and he took the odd will and conveyance case that he ran through the company books. Croswitz handled mostly personal injury, specializing in car wrecks. He looked a thousand years old and avoided juries like the plague.

The office was small and clean, but empty. I knocked, then knocked again, then wandered in and rang the bell that sat on the reception desk. Nothing. So I walked in and knocked on the private office, then opened the door. Croswitz was asleep at his desk, head back, mouth open. I might have thought he was dead, except for the guttural snore that shook the bookshelves. I didn't want to give the old fossil a heart attack, so I poked him gently, with no response. I took a stack of legal journals from a bookcase and dropped them onto his desk. He stirred at the impact, smacked his lips together, then opened his eyes.

"Miami, I didn't hear you come in," he said, as if he had been studying the legal journals I'd thrown in front of him. He wiped his mouth and rubbed his eyes. "How are you?"

"Not bad. Just got shot at."

"Well, that's something. What can I do for you?"

"Your girl in today?" I smiled. Maybe at his age you got away with calling your receptionist your girl, but I knew if I tried that with Lizzy, she would tear me a new one.

"No," he said, leaning back in his chair. "She's only in two days a week. Why?"

"I need to sue somebody. Today."

Croswitz nodded like this was not an unusual request. "I have a boilerplate on the computer. I can call my wife's nephew to take the papers over to the courthouse. He's useless for most things, but he can deliver papers."

"Can he serve them on the defendant?"

"Sure," nodded the old guy. "This isn't going to trial, is it?" he said, suddenly concerned.

"Not even close."

Croswitz smiled his yellow grin.

I left him to enter the names and dates on his boilerplate document, and I headed up to my office. Lizzy sat at her desk, typing something that I didn't need to know about. She looked at me, then narrowed her eyes.

"There was gunfire down in the parking lot," she said.

"Yeah, I know," I said.

"I'm going to need danger pay if that keeps up."

"Just don't leave the office with me," I said, smiling.

I went into my office and poured three fingers of Scotch and lay back on the sofa. I didn't feel good. I was halfway between hungover and healthy, and although my doctor might not have agreed with my chosen remedy, the Scotch did take the edge off. I was thinking about the Boston guys, about them losing their jobs. I wasn't sure if it was because of the beating we gave them, or the money, or the fact that we had taken out the van as a result. Either way, with Baldy down for the count and Redhead off to the morgue, it was good odds on not getting a repeat visit.

Ron burst into my office, a frown of concern plastered across his face. He pointed out the window.

"You?" he said.

I nodded and sipped.

"I didn't realize you were carrying these days," he said, dropping in the seat behind my desk.

"I'm not. The cops took that guy down."

"The officer in charge seemed miffed you'd left the scene."

"He knows where to find me."

We chatted while I finished my Scotch, then I put the glass on the floor and closed my eyes. When I woke the sun had almost gone, and I was startled by Lizzy coming into the room. Ron was still behind my desk, but he seemed to have gotten himself a coffee and finished it.

"A package for you," she said. "A kid from Croswitz and Allen just dropped it off."

I swung my feet onto the floor and sat up. Lizzy handed me the package and wandered out. I took it and ripped it open. There was a note, along with some papers and a jewel case with a CD inside. The note was from Jenny Almondson.

Miami, thought I'd hear from you, so here is a copy of what I have. Sorry, JA.

"What is it?" asked Ron.

"The evidence against Julio."

"How did that happen so fast? I thought you said Croswitz's nephew was going to serve the papers this afternoon?" asked Ron.

"I asked him to serve her before he went to the courthouse. Clearly, Jenny Almondson was expecting it. She had this ready to go."

I dropped the CD into the tray and pressed play. As it began spinning around I looked at the papers. They were an executive summary of what was on the CD and why. The summary detailed how, as per Florida gaming regulations, Casino Director of Security George Finau undertook an investigation into alleged improprieties in the gaming on jai alai after receiving an anonymous tipoff. As part of the inquiry, Finau hired a local private investigator, Max Stubbs, who discovered potential unsanctioned betting practices by Diego Alvarez, better known as Julio. The report said Stubbs met with Julio under the guise of an illegal bookmaker, wearing a wire. The following pages were a transcript of the highlights of their conversation. I stopped reading and listened as the recording kicked in. There was a lot of background noise, like they were at a party, or the mall.

Stubbs: "The question is, can you deliver the results we need?"

Julio: "Of course."

Stubbs: "Can you offer spreads, or just wins in specified games?"

Julio: "Wins. The other, this will cost more."

Stubbs: "Cost is not the issue. If you can fix the results we need, we'll get the bets on, and you and your boys will get your cut."

Julio: "We can deliver exactly what you want."

Stubbs: "Good. This envelope has a down payment. Five hundred. Deliver us a win for Miguel in the first game on Tuesday, by two points. You do that, we can do more business. Okay?"

Julio: "It will be done."

Ron flipped open the laptop on my desk and tapped at the keys as I finished reading the report. Stubbs had provided the evidence to Finau, who had reported it to Almondson. She had consulted with the casino's attorneys and, as a result, had met with Julio. The outcome of that meeting had been Julio's dismissal.

"Okay, Tuesday last," said Ron. He ran his finger down the screen and frowned, then looked at me.

"Miguel won the first game by two points."

I leaned back against the sofa and put my hands on my head. "So are we representing a cheat?"

Ron copied my lean back and hands on head, then added pouting lips. "I don't get it."

"Don't get what?"

"Fixing jai alai isn't this easy. One guy can't really do it," said Ron.

"That's what Roto said."

"I remember back in the day, there was always a lot of talk about how the game was crooked, but no one ever really figured a way. One guy doesn't dominate play enough. It's not one on one, it's one on seven, and any of those seven could upset your plan, so you'd almost need them all in."

"Could they all be in it?" I said. "I mean, I can't imagine a jai alai player earns that much. This must be tempting."

"They earn more than you think," said Ron. "Back in the eighties it was big money, but even now I think they have a base salary plus prize money. It comes in around seventy grand a year."

"Not too shabby."

Ron shook his head. "What do you know about the casino manager?" he asked.

"Jenny? She's a looker—just don't tell Danielle I said that. But she seems to support the jai alai, even if it is begrudgingly. She acknowledged it was a necessary cross to bear to be in business. She even beefed up security after the initial threats."

"What about the security guy?"

"Finau? Big unit. Samoan, Tongan, something like that. Doesn't say much. Doesn't have to. After the threats it looks like Jenny had him bring in some of his own people. They create a presence, that's for sure. Which makes me think, do you know anything about this PI, Stubbs? I don't know him."

Ron nodded and picked up the phone. "I've heard of him, but Lizzy will know more."

Ron called Lizzy and she came back in with something that could almost pass for a smile. Ron had that effect on her. I had the opposite effect. Her hair was the color of coal, and her pale face was made even whiter by the shock of red lipstick that seemed permanently tattooed on her lips. She looked like the kind of woman who might beat her husband, regardless of his size, but she had no such relationship. Jesus, she said, was the only man in her life. Ron asked her to sit with us, and she took a visitor's chair by my desk.

"Do you know of a PI called Stubbs, Max Stubbs?" said Ron.

Lizzy pouted her lips and frowned. "Aha, yeah, I've heard of him. Not the most discreet guy you'll meet. Word is he'll take any case, and get whatever result you need. I've heard he's good for telling whatever story you need on the stand. Perjury doesn't seem to faze him." She shook her head and snarled. "I can't abide that."

"Lying under oath?" said Ron.

"With your hand on the Bible. That's lying to God." She shook her head again.

"Sounds like he'd sell out his mother for a cheap steak dinner," I said.

Lizzy turned to me on the sofa. "He'd sell her out for a salad."

Ron and I both grimaced at the idea of getting sold out for a bowl of greens.

"Do you know where he works out of, Lizzy?" I said.

"He's got an office out near the turnpike, on Okeechobee Boulevard, if I recall."

I looked at Ron and he at me.

"Field trip tomorrow?" he said.

CHAPTER TWENTY—FIVE

Having a low-rent office in a strip mall in South Florida is no sign of anything. Lots of decent businesses have such offices, mainly because there are a lot of strip malls, and the rent is cheap. But even as far as strip malls went, this one was a doozy. The parking lot had been cracked and faded to the color of ash by the constant beating of the sun. The tenants were a choice collection of pawn shops, check cashing outlets, and a liquor store whose claim to fame seemed to be that it had sold a winning ticket in the state lottery, back in 1999. At least I was dressed for the occasion, in cargo shorts and my blue palm tree motif shirt. Stubbs's office was at the end of the row, windows tinted with peeling, silver reflective panels. My busted SUV had been moved from the crime scene to an auto shop, so I parked the tiny Korean rental at the other end of the strip, and Ron and I walked by the storefronts to the PI's office.

A little bell dinged as we stepped inside, like a convenience store. The height of security. Stubbs was nowhere to be seen. The office was sparsely furnished with drab, well-used items. Desks that looked like hand-me-downs from the Department of Corrections, vinyl chairs that were universally splitting, a ragged sofa and fake plants that were the color of dust. A battalion of tiny ants marched along the skirting board. We heard a flushing sound and a door opened at the rear of the space. A man built like a beanbag waddled out, waving a newspaper at his behind. He appeared to be sweating, as if he'd just run a half marathon. He got to his desk before he noticed us, then he dropped the paper on the desk and jutted out his chin.

"Help you?" he said.

"Looking for Max Stubbs," I said.

"You found him." Stubbs bobbled forward and stuck out a moist paw. I looked at the hand but declined to shake it. Dysentery seemed like a real possibility.

"My name is Miami Jones," I said instead. Stubbs dropped his hand, not seemingly put out by the rebuke. He frowned like he was trying to place me at a high school reunion.

"I know you, don't I?"

"I don't believe we've ever met," I said.

"Yeah, I know you. I seen you in the papers. The Miami Jones. You did that case for BJ Baker. Found his Heisman trophy."

"That we did."

"You do a lot of work in Palm Beach?" he said.

"Some. You?"

He shook his head and puckered his face. "Not really my scene."

No, indeed. Stubbs didn't offer us a seat or a coffee, though I would probably have declined both, on health grounds.

"What do you guys want?" said Stubbs, cutting to the chase.

"You recently did some work for the West Palm Jai Alai and Casino."

Stubbs shrugged. "Did I?"

"Yes, you did. Impersonating an illegal bookmaker. Ring any bells?"

Stubbs frowned. "What is it you want?"

"We're curious about that case. How you came to discover that Diego Alvarez was open to illegal betting."

"They're all open to it. It's jai alai, isn't it?"

"You watch a lot of jai alai?"

"Nup. I only watch real sports. American sports."

"Well, I can appreciate that," I said. "But had you known more about jai alai, you might know that it is virtually impossible for one man to fix a game."

"So they were all in on it. What of it?"

"Why did you focus on Diego Alvarez?"

"Look, I'm not talking about this with you. It's none of your goddamned business."

"We represent Mr. Alvarez, so actually it is very much our business."

"Represent him? For what? You ain't lawyers."

I looked at Ron. "We're not lawyers?"

"No, technically you have to pass the bar," said Ron.

"Is that so?"

"And go to law school."

"All right, smart guys," Stubbs said. "I know when I'm being made fun of. You think because you come over from the island that you're so much better than me."

"No," I said. "I think I'm better than you because I bathe regularly."

"Get out," said Stubbs, stepping toward me. He was a big guy, but there are different versions of big. George Finau was big in a muscular, imposing way. I was big in that I was head and shoulders taller than Stubbs. Stubbs was big in the way Australia was big. All girth, no height. He stepped to me so his belly touched my shirt, but he wasn't nearly as scary as he thought he was.

"I said get out, fancy boy."

It had been a long time since I had been called fancy while wearing a shirt with palm trees on it, so I smiled. Stubbs tried to snarl, but it looked more like a facial spasm, and it was unpleasant to watch, so I turned away to the door.

"Later, Stubbs," I said.

Ron held the door open, and the bell rang, and we walked back out into the million-dollar sunshine.

"What do you think?" I asked Ron.

"He's a real snake in the grass, but that doesn't prove anything. Not everyone in this profession is as pleasant as you," he said.

"Or you, good sir."

We got into the rental car, and Ron turned to me. "Do you think he's up to no good?"

I nodded. "On a regular basis. But specifically related to our case? Not sure. I do have one nagging question, though."

"And that is?" said Ron, as I pulled out of the lot and back onto Okeechobee Boulevard.

"Did that look like a high-tech operation to you?"

Ron frowned. "It looked like a refugee camp to me."

"Exactly. Yet the evidence was burned onto a CD. With a label printed directly on it. I don't think that falls into Mr. Stubbs's skill set, do you?"

"Anyone can burn a CD. It's not that hard."

"It's the printed label that got me. It looked like a pro job, not an ink jet and some craft glue."

"I see what you're saying. So Stubbs had the CD done up. But what does that mean?"

"It means there was someone else involved," I said. "And I want to know who."

CHAPTER TWENTY–SIX

Ron and I lunched at Longboard Kelly's. I stayed with iced tea, as I was waiting for Lucas to arrive and couldn't be sure what the afternoon might hold. Ron took the rental car back to the office to do some digging into Max Stubbs, and I sat and watched Muriel polish glasses until Lucas arrived. We took his beat-up Tacoma pickup down A1A, to a seventies special office block just south of the airport. We had gotten the address from the unlucky driver of the bookie's van. The building was two stories with a facade of concrete mixed with crushed coral and seashells. The vacant lot next door was covered in grass sun-bleached the color of dead wheat, and the other side was a vacant storefront that looked like it had once been a cocktail lounge. The ground floor of the office we wanted was made up like a travel agency—lots of posters for places like Prague and Fiji. I didn't realize that travel agents like that still existed, which made me think the whole thing was a front. I paused on the street before the door.

"You don't need to do this, you know," I said. "Desi is safe now."

Lucas didn't look at me; he just stretched his neck to look up at the building.

"As long as these guys are still here, there'll always be another Desi. It's something every government I ever took orders from didn't get. You can't just snip the top off a weed and walk away. You have pull it out, roots and all. Otherwise it grows back."

We took the stairs on the side of the building to the upper floor. The reception area was humid, more so than outside, and smelled of cigars. A young guy in shirtsleeves sat behind a heavy wooden desk. He eyed us as though his distance vision was less than 20/20, but said nothing.

"We're looking for Mr. Barrett," I said.

The guy made a face and shrugged.

"No one by that name here," he said.

"And your name is?"

"I don't got a name," he said.

"I tell you what," I said, but before I could continue Lucas strode to the door leading back to the offices and pulled at it. It didn't open. The guy at the desk gave a grin like there was some kind of secret password required, and he knew it, but wasn't sharing. Lucas, however, had his own password. He stepped back, then kicked at the lock once, twice and on the third shot smashed the knob. Lucas slipped the knob out of the hole and used the hole to pull open the door. The guy at the desk stood, mouth open like a trawling net, but did nothing more. Obviously his squinting drove off most unwanted visitors.

Lucas charged down a hallway of worn carpet flanked by office doors, some of which flew open, but no one made a move toward him. I dashed through and kept on his hip. All the faces looked like accountants, not mobsters. Rolled-up shirtsleeves, loosened ties. At the end of the hall was another door, and it flew open, and a big guy in a cheap suit stepped out.

"No," was all he said, and he marched right at Lucas. I thought for a moment he was going to pull a gun, but he didn't. It seemed like he was pretty confident he could solve problems without one, and I wasn't completely sure he was wrong.

"Mr. Barrett," said Lucas.

The big guy shook his head. "Not happening."

They reached each other in the narrow hallway like jousters, at less than full pace but still no one giving any quarter. The big guy put his fists up and propped, ready for a fight. Lucas didn't reciprocate. He kept moving, then he drove the heel of his palm into the guy's breast plate, knocking the wind out of him. The guy collapsed backward like a fallen pine tree, and Lucas stepped over him and continued into the office. I hurdled the guy struggling to suck back a breath and followed Lucas in.

The office wasn't large, but it was nicer than the rest of the place. The desk was polished rosewood, and the real houseplants were well cared for. The vertical blinds were drawn, keeping out the wonderful winter sun, so the only light came from a desk lamp. The guy behind the desk was olive-skinned and dark. Deep-set eyes watched us enter from under heavy eyebrows. He looked neither shocked nor pleased with the kerfuffle we were causing. Lucas stepped into the room and positioned himself away from the door, at forty-five degrees to the desk.

"You Barrett?" said Lucas.

"Who wants to know?" said the guy.

"I do. You think I'm here for the good of my health?"

"I think we can be certain that your health is of no concern to you."

The guy had one of those homogenous accents that could have been from the Midwest, or even the West Coast. A television accent.

"All right, mate. I am going to assume you are Barrett. If it turns out you are not and I have wasted my time, I am going to beat your face to a pulp until your own mum couldn't recognize you. Got me?"

"Sounds ugly."

"You've been taking bets in a van at the West Palm Jai Alai," said Lucas.

A crease of recognition flashed over the man's face.

"You are the man who hurt my employees," he said.

"Your employees hurt themselves," said Lucas, "the moment they decided to take bets from underage kids."

Barrett shook his head slowly.

"We do no such thing. We provide opportunity. People want to play, who are you to say they can't? This is a free country."

"These are not just people, they're children. You're taking money from kids who can barely afford to eat, and then you're throwing them in the ocean when they can't pay." Lucas's face was contorted with barely suppressed rage at the thought of Desi in the water.

"Listen, my friend, I don't want any trouble. And I don't want anyone killed. That isn't good for business. Dead people never pay. I like live bait, you see? Live people play, and they pay. We might have to help them remember their obligations, but nothing serious. I want them around to play again."

"Your guys threw a boy in the ocean."

"Those boys no longer work for me," said Barrett. The office door creaked as the big guy from the hallway staggered in, still short of breath but looking for a fight. Barrett put his hand up to hold the guy in place.

"Look, like I said, I don't want trouble unless I want trouble. Good help is hard to find. Those boys overstepped without authority, and now they are no longer part of my organization. So I suggest you take your beef to the gym and work it out on a bag, because no good can come from me ever seeing you again."

Lucas stood tall and breathed in and out.

"What a man does is his business, his responsibility," said Lucas. "But when you take money from children, when you hurt them, then you overstep. So leave the kids alone."

Barrett smiled. It wasn't a pleasant smile.

"My friend, this is America. It's a free country. So I'll run my business however I please. If little illegal runts want to wash their money away, that's not my problem. And neither are you. You've made your big statement, smashed into my place like Rambo. So now let me tell you something. I see your face again, you're dead. If I hear you've been near my people, you're dead. You show your face at the fronton, you're dead. You are not a customer, you don't play. So I really don't mind if you are dead."

Lucas and Barrett stared each other down, then Lucas relaxed his shoulders. I waited for the storm to come, for him to explode into action. But he shrugged and walked out, past the big guy in the doorway. I followed, wondering what his plan was, as we ambled down the stairs and back onto the street. Lucas said nothing all the way back to his truck. Once we got in, I watched him. He seemed calm, serene even. My heart was almost pumping out of my chest.

"What do you think?" I said.

Lucas shrugged.

"I learned a long time ago, mate, some fellas can't be reasoned with. No point getting worked up about it— that's just how they are."

"So that's it?"

He looked at me and smiled.

"Christ, no. When a fella won't hear reason, then you just gotta get unreasonable."

I nodded. I had no idea what that meant, but I got the feeling it was something like a pitcher deciding to throw at the batter's head, on purpose.

"So what now?" I said.

"Now I gotta get back to the marina. I got two big boats visiting that both want a full clean and pull through."

"No, I mean about Barrett?"

"Oh, him. I reckon we let him sweat a little bit more. 'Sides, I've got a boat delivery I gotta do. I'm gonna be away for a couple days. I'll catch you when I get back. Righto?"

I didn't answer. It didn't feel like a question, but with Lucas it was hard to tell. He dropped me near the courthouse and pulled away toward the freeway with a wave of his hand. I wandered back around the parking lot where the police tape had been removed and everything was back to normal. But nothing felt normal. Lucas was backing from a fight, I hadn't spoken to Danielle in days, and when I got to the office I learned Ron had taken off to see Cassandra in Palm Beach. I didn't even go to my desk. I told Lizzy I was heading out, and she said that was fine, like her whole life revolved around my movements. I tossed up going to Longboard's, but without Ron or Danielle, I lacked the energy for it. Then my phone rang. It was Ron.

"Cassandra's got a friend who needs some strong hands to help sail her boat for a twilight sail tonight. Peel and eats, champers included. You in?"

"Not sure I'm great company right now, Ron."

"Come on, come get some of those negative ions in you. Besides, her husband is in New York, and I can't work all the sheets myself."

"And the girls can't help?"

"What are you thinking? I can't ask Palm Beach ladies to do the heavy lifting. That's what guys like you and I are for."

I couldn't work up a rebuttal so I said I'd be there in half an hour, and I got in the tiny rental car and headed out over the bridge, to pull some ropes and clear my head.

CHAPTER TWENTY—SEVEN

I totally get why rich people sail. There's something invigorating about feeling that salty breeze in your face, doing a little manual work, pulling sheets and trimming sails, and then following the effort up with a glass of bubbly at sunset. That's my kind of sailing. None of this offshore, big waves, no-land-in-sight garbage. Ron was right; I felt much better after the sail, and as we tied up back at the docks at the end of Australian Avenue, I came to the conclusion that I was overthinking things. Time would reveal the solutions, with a little prodding. We enjoyed a few drinks on board at the docks, then Ron led a group to adjourn to Cassandra's apartment, a short walk across the island. I declined, with the excuse that I had to drive home, and offered to wash down the deck. I grabbed a hose and wandered around the white deck, washing the salt back into the Intracoastal. As I was coiling the hose I felt the vibration in the dock of the approach of multiple footsteps. I looked up to see two guys in slick, thin-cut suits standing before me. I wondered whose black cat I had driven over to warrant another set of hoods visiting me, and although neither guy's slim-fit suit left anything to the imagination, I couldn't discount firearms.

"Miami Jones," said a guy in a clipped Brooklyn accent. The accent didn't tell me everything. There were so many New Yorkers in Palm Beach during the season, it was like living on Long Island Sound. But not too many converts wore custom-tailored pinstripe suits.

"You boys lost?" I said, holding the end of the hose in my hand as if the guys would be afraid to get wet.

"Mr. Hoskin hasn't heard from you," said guy one, the shorter of the two.

I frowned. I certainly recalled Elroy Hoskin offering me undiscussed benefits to keep him updated on the lowdown regarding his proposed casino, but I didn't recall accepting the job.

"Mr. Hoskin wanted to remind you that he values his friendships very highly."

"That's nice of him to send you guys down to say that. Most people would just call."

"It's important to him that you understand the quid pro quo involved."

I wondered if those had been Hoskin's words or if henchmen were now required to have a college education.

"Mr. Hoskin wonders why he hasn't heard from you."

"Mr. Hoskin hasn't heard from me because I only met him a couple nights ago, I haven't got anything to say to him, and I don't have a duo of well-dressed baboons at my pleasure to send him a pointless message."

The silent guy didn't flinch, but the one with the gift of speech got the barb, and I saw his jawline tighten. "You'd do well to remember your place, mister."

I laughed, a real, good old gut-giggle. I love it when rich people suggest I remember my standing in their totem, as if I was actually part of their damned hierarchy in the first place. And I especially enjoyed the irony of them sending that message through their minions.

"Are you serious? Unlike you pair of clotheshorses, I don't have a place to remember. I don't work for Hoskin, regardless of what he thinks. So if, and I mean if, I hear something useful, I will decide at that time whether or not I can be bothered to pass it on to him. And at this point, I am not particularly inclined to do so."

The speech-capable baboon processed this message and grinned. "He thought you'd say that. He knows things are happening, and you haven't provided anything useful. So he said we should offer you a reminder."

He took a step forward and the backup baboon seemed to come alive at the smell of blood.

"You're kidding me, right? Hoskin wants to give me a beating for not calling a couple days after we met? Doesn't he understand playing hard to get?"

"He said you were the kind of smart guy who would respond well to 'physical persuasion', and not much else. So we're here to give it to you."

"Does that ever work? Telling people you're about to beat them up? Kind of loses the element of surprise, doesn't it?" I said.

"Where you going to go?" smiled Baboon One.

It was a fair point. I was at the end of a dock, with water one way and a beating on the other. But I knew that. I was buying time. The guys moved toward me, and when they got close enough, I punched open the lever on the dock hose, hitting them with a jet of high-pressure water. Despite the fact I'd had the hose in my hand the whole time, they weren't prepared for the spraying, and they both recoiled as their fancy duds got soaked. But I knew the effect was limited. They weren't actually going to go down, and eventually they would meet the intersection of can't-get-any-wetter and very annoyed, at which point they'd be coming hard. The first guy came fast, but he was restricted in his tight suit—which was a stunning look, but not recommended boxing apparel— and the suit jacket ripped as he cocked his arm back. I didn't wait for impact, dropping the hose and jumping back up onto the yacht. The guy struggled to get on the boat, and his buddy, who had taken a moment to discard his jacket, beat him to it. He came at me, and I moved toward the pointy end of the deck. The backup baboon had trouble getting traction on the wet deck in his loafers, and he grabbed at some wire stays to hold himself up.

That was my cue. I stepped forward and kicked him right in the gut, sending him crashing over the gunwale and into the water. There wasn't a whole lot of room between dock spaces, so he slammed hard into the hull of the yacht next door as he fell. I took a second to check that he was still conscious and wasn't going to drown, and it was a second too long. Baboon One launched himself into a full-on body tackle. We both went crashing to the deck and started sliding down toward the lifelines. My shoulder crunched into a stanchion, and the baboon slid into me. He tried throwing punches, but between the tight suit and slippery deck, he didn't have much success. I held him off until he used up a good dose of energy, then I slid out from under him and grabbed a stay and lifted myself up.

"Enough already," I said, puffing.

But he clearly took his job seriously and wasn't giving up so easily. He dragged himself up and finally tore away his jacket, then gingerly moved forward. At this point I was over the whole episode, so I used my sartorial advantage. I charged at the guy and tackled him. I went to University of Miami on a football scholarship, so I could lay a tackle. Granted, I was a quarterback, so it wasn't a bone cruncher or anything, but we both went flying over the edge of the deck anyway, landing right on top of the other baboon who was floating there, holding his head. The two guys started flapping like spawning salmon. They were in suits and clearly didn't swim much. I swam at City Beach on a regular basis, and I was wearing shorts and deck shoes, so I took a deep breath and went down under the hull. It was further than I thought, and my chest was burning by the time I felt the middle of the hull turn upward, so I kicked hard and exploded up on the other side of the yacht. I figured from that point I could outswim them if I had to. But I didn't have to, because at that moment I heard the burble of a police siren. I grabbed onto the post at the end of the dock and felt the steady beat of multiple sets of feet marching forward again.

"Get those two out of there," said a voice, clearly in command, and I felt my stocks take a dive. Footsteps in my direction and I looked up to see a face appear from the dock. The face of Palm Beach detective and my part-time nemesis, Detective Ronzoni. Ronzoni took a moment to clarify what he was looking at.

Then he smiled, like the cat that had just gotten the cream.

CHAPTER TWENTY–EIGHT

"You really are in a whole world of hurt," said Ronzoni, as he paced before me. I sat on a dock box, sans towel, shivering in the twilight. Ronzoni prowled like a toddler in need of the bathroom. He wore his trademark wrinkled Sears wrinkle-free suit, and a tie covered in the kind of paisley I hadn't seen since the seventies. He was thin and wiry, except for his belly, which was a bulb that pushed at his tie. He was enjoying himself.

"See, Jones, it's simple math. Two against one. These gentlemen say you attacked them, and seeing as you don't have any witnesses . . ." He smiled at the thought. We both knew there was nothing that could stick, but he'd enjoy putting me in the lockup for the night.

"You do that math yourself, Zamboni?"

"It's Ronzoni, meatball, and even you can't harsh my mellow. This is too good."

"Those guys were sent by Elroy Hoskin. It doesn't worry you that he's bringing New York action to Palm Beach?"

"Mr. Hoskin is a guest on the island," said Ronzoni. "What's your excuse?"

"Same, pretty much. But Hoskin thinks this is how you do things here. Is that right? You going to let this kind of thing happen on the island? Don't think the residents will be very pleased with that."

"No, I am not going to let that kind of thing happen on the island. I am going to put you in lockup, and tomorrow I am going to escort you off the island as far as the bridge. You can walk to the impound to get your car from there."

"My car's not in impound," I said.

"Not yet," smiled Ronzoni.

Touché.

I couldn't have wiped the smile off his face with an electric sander, but then his phone rang. He took the call with his back to me. "Yes, Chief. Aha. Yes, sir, he's here."

Ronzoni glanced over his shoulder, and as he did, I saw the bubble deflate. "But, sir," he said.

He spun and took several steps away from me. "Yes, but sir. There are witnesses. Yes, sir, they are together. No, sir, they have no reason to be on the dock. No, sir. Yes, sir. Yes, sir." He ended the call and stood slack-shouldered, then took a deep breath, then slowly turned back to me.

"Three bags full?" I smiled.

"You have more lives than a rabid cat," he said. His suit suddenly looked too big for him. "That was the chief. Seems like the dock security that called in the disturbance also called the owner of the yacht you were on. Seems she was at a party at your friend Lady Cassandra's, and when they heard you were in custody they called the chief."

I smiled. "Some days you're the Louisville Slugger, some days you're the ball."

A modicum of joy came back to Ronzoni's face. "Chief said to let her dock boy go. So you can go, dock boy."

I considered giving some cheek back but thought better of it. He wasn't a bad guy; he was just a poorly paid cop doing his job in one of the ritziest places in the country. Having your face rubbed in it like that everyday could give you a real *Upstairs, Downstairs* mentality. I patted him on the shoulder as I stood.

"Maybe you'll win the next one," I said.

He nodded.

"Just don't bet on it." I smiled as I walked away into the night.

I dried off in Cassandra's bathroom and then joined the impromptu party I had planned on skipping. I regaled everyone with details of events, then the conversation drifted away as people added their own anecdotes about the time they did this or the time they saw that. I was okay with it. The spotlight wasn't my favorite place to be.

Despite years as a professional pitcher, I never coveted the bright lights. On the mound I was in a cocoon, a bubble where I blocked out the noise and crowd and chitchat coming from the batter and just did my thing. But win or lose, after the game, I would take to the shadows and let the other guys tell the stories about the games, to girls in bars or guys in trucks, or just to each other. As the conversation flowed I drifted outside onto the massive deck. There was a breeze coming in off the ocean, and it was as cold as it gets in South Florida. I could almost have gone for pants. Almost. I heard the door slide open and closed, and Ron appeared at my side. We stood looking at the waves breaking on the beach in the moonlight.

"You okay, *Kemosabe*?" asked Ron.

"Just fine."

"Interesting evening."

"You could say."

Ron sipped his drink, then looked at me. "Why is Hoskin so twitchy?" he said.

"I don't know. But you are right. He's twitchy. Maybe he's just used to getting it all his own way in Vegas, and he's not taking kindly to Palm Beach thumbing its nose at him. I was a convenient whipping boy for his annoyance."

We stared out at the ocean again for a time, then Ron's phone bleeped from his pocket. He smiled at the screen and winked at me.

"Well, hello, Deputy Castle."

I stood upright at Danielle's name. I hadn't spoken to her since she had left for Atlanta.

"No, his phone is a little out of commission right now," said Ron. "But he can explain himself. He's right here."

Ron handed me his phone with a smile and turned to go inside. I leaned on the balcony and put the phone to my ear.

"Hey, you," I said.

"Back at you," she said. She sounded good. She could have worked in telemarketing and made a bundle with that voice.

"Sorry I haven't caught you," I said. "How's it going?"

"Actually, it's going pretty great."

"Yeah? Tell me."

"Well, I'm learning a lot. The latest theories on law enforcement, new techniques, all that."

"Sounds like a hoot."

"But that's not the best part. Everyone here is pretty senior, and of course they know that I'm just filling in for the boss, but that doesn't seem to matter. When we're workshopping, or even just chatting at the bar, they all listen to my opinion, as if it were just as valid as any of theirs."

"It is just as valid," I said.

"Yeah, I guess so. But it feels like it's validated somehow. Like I belong here. Like I could offer more than just being a deputy."

"You could be more, so good for you."

"Really, you think so? You never said that before."

"I haven't?"

In that moment I realized that it was true. I hadn't said it, because I hadn't seen it. I saw Danielle as my lover, my partner, a sharer of sunsets and good times. And when she left for work in her uniform, I saw her as a deputy. A damn good-looking one, for sure, but a deputy nevertheless. I knew she could be more. She was smarter than the average bear, and tenacious and caring and resourceful. But it occurred to me that I might not have said those things. That I might have assumed them to be facts in evidence and taken them for granted.

Taken her for granted.

"Well, if I haven't," I said, "I'm saying it now. I'm glad it's going well."

"How about you? Did you get anywhere with Desi?"

"It's been an interesting few days. But yes, we found out who was behind the betting ring that snared little Desi."

"Did you report it to the office?"

"Sort of."

"MJ?"

"You knew we had a word with the guys who hurt Desi."

"Yes, and I'd like to have more than a word," she said.

"Not necessary. They sort of came after me."

"Oh, no. Are you okay?"

"Yes, I'm fine. The two idiots tried to take me down in the office parking lot."

"That lot doesn't seem to be very good luck for you," she said.

"No, but this time it had its benefits."

"Like being right across from the courthouse?"

"Exactly. The West Palm PD took down one of the guys, and the other is in custody."

There was silence on the line, and I waited until I thought we'd been cut off.

"Danielle? You there?"

"Yes," she said softly. "Just be careful."

"I'm always careful, sweetheart."

I decided to not mention the visit to El Tiburon, or the van, or the little altercation with Hoskin's guys in Palm Beach. She didn't sound ready to hear about that.

"Listen, I have to go, I'm meeting some people for drinks."

"You bet. Enjoy. I'm just here, hanging out at Cassandra's," I said.

"No picking up some wealthy heiress," she said.

I smiled. "I thought I'd already done that."

Danielle laughed. "You chose poorly," she said. "I love you. I'll call again before I head back."

"Love you, too. Go impress the pants off them. Well, not the pants. You know what I mean."

"I do. See you soon."

I looked back over the ocean, and it wasn't long before Ron wandered back out.

"All okay?" he said.

"All good. Sounds like she's having a great time. Networking, all that jazz."

"Good stuff."

I handed Ron his phone.

"I need to get a new phone," I said. "Mine's waterlogged."

"Fix that tomorrow. Let's get you a drink. Cassandra has a room all set up for you to stay."

"That's generous, but I have something I need to do first. Should only take an hour."

"I'll come with you," said Ron.

"No, you enjoy the party."

"Like you said, it'll just be an hour. Besides," he said, smiling at me, "a man should never commit breaking and entering alone."

CHAPTER TWENTY—NINE

The strip malls on Okeechobee Boulevard don't look any better at night. At least not out near the turnpike. Half the lights were busted, so there were plenty of dark shadows. Unfortunately the light out front of the offices of Max Stubbs, Private Investigator, was burning brightly. I dashed around the back to check the rear entrance but found two decent deadlocks. The front door, however, was a flimsy aluminum frame around glass and had a lock to match. We could have broken it easy enough, but first preference was to leave no trace of our having been there. I played lookout, and Ron got down on his knees and picked the lock. Traffic wasn't too heavy, and most people were focused on the upcoming ramp onto the turnpike, so we took the chance that passersby would pay us no mind. Ron had a few drinks in him, so it took a little longer than was comfortable, but with a giggle he got the lock open. Clad in latex gloves, we entered like cat burglars. The little bell rang, reminding me again of an old general store. I locked the door behind us, to give us at least some warning if someone—particularly Stubbs himself—appeared. Ron scanned the room with a flashlight, finding the same disheveled space: a matted sofa, a filing cabinet, and a desk with a computer monitor sitting on it. The main drawer of the cabinet was locked, but the key was sitting in the upper drawer for anyone who cared to look. I flicked through the files but found nothing related to casinos or jai alai.

"His computer is on," said Ron.

I turned to see Ron's face glowing in the light of the monitor. I edged through the darkness to join him at the screen that was showing a fireworks display.

"Password?" I said.

Ron wobbled the computer mouse with his hand; the fireworks dissolved, and a desktop appeared. "Doesn't appear to have a password," he said.

"This guy is not exactly Fort Knox, is he?"

"Who can remember all these passwords, anyway?" said Ron.

He clicked around the screen, looking through files but finding nothing of interest. He opened the email application and looked through the communications. It seemed Stubbs worked a lot of divorce cases and had accepted in-kind payment from a number of jilted wives. But there was nothing that helped us.

"Maybe he didn't keep records," said Ron.

"No, he doesn't seem like the record-keeping type. But there's a difference between keeping records and there being records." I leaned in to the screen and glanced at Ron. "May I?"

Ron gave me control of the computer, and I moved the cursor to the little trash can and clicked on it. The screen filled with emails, those sent and received that Stubbs didn't wish to keep. He had trashed them, only he hadn't deleted them. Lizzy had shown me the same thing once when I thought I had gotten rid of some emails. She'd said a forensic IT team could get at the data even after it was deleted, but simply moving it to the trash just left it in the trash. Just like in my kitchen, the trash can didn't empty itself.

I read through some of the email headings until I found one titled *Re: audio edit*. I clicked on it. The email was from someone called Dexter at a free email account. Dexter had apparently done the edits requested by Stubbs and had attached the finished file. I clicked on the attachment, and it opened in a media player. I recognized the scratchy background noise straight away. It was the recording of Julio making the fix with Stubbs. I didn't need to hear it all again, so as soon as I heard Julio's voice I clicked it closed and went back to the emails. I found all the other emails to and from Dexter. Some of them related to other cases. One email instructed Stubbs on how to download the audio files from his recording device, which was followed by an exchange of emails that detailed Stubbs attempting to do this without success.

The final email was from an exasperated Dexter, telling Stubbs to drop the device off at the recording studio and to trash all their email correspondence.

I waited while Ron finished reading the email, then we looked at each other and smiled. But our smiles dropped when we heard the sound of keys jangling at the front door. I clicked the email application closed as Ron hit the button to turn off the monitor. For a moment the room glowed and the screen stayed determinedly bright, and the key slid into the lock and turned. The little bell rang, and we heard a giggle that definitely hadn't come from Stubbs. Then the monitor died. Ron and I dropped below the desk, blinded by the sudden darkness. We were blinded again by the burst of fluorescent light as the switch was flicked on.

"Here we are, my darling," said Stubbs.

I blinked hard and waited for Stubbs to wander into the room and find us crouched behind his desk. I suddenly wished I'd worn a ski mask like a proper cat burglar.

"I'm not your darling, Max. And this is way too bright. Don't you have any candles?" said a woman.

"Candles?" said Max. "What for?"

"For crying out loud, Max. If not for ambience, how about hurricanes?"

"I wouldn't stay in here during a hurricane, darling."

"Just turn the lights off, and let's get this done."

Once more the room plunged into darkness, blinding us again. My pupils were working so hard I felt faint, but at least now everyone had night blindness. The door slammed itself closed. I heard Stubbs and the woman fumble their way toward us. Someone, Stubbs by the weight of it, put a hand on the desk, and it moved slightly.

"Where?" said the woman.

"Here," said Stubbs. "Right here."

We heard the pfft sound of bodies collapsing on the sofa.

"Ow, watch it," said the woman.

"Sorry, darling," said Stubbs. "Now why don't you come here?"

"No, Max. You lay back. I've got this."

We heard rustling in the darkness, and I felt the growing desire to retch. Then the unmistakable sound of a zipper being pulled.

"Yeah, baby. You're a bad girl."

"Shut up, Max. Just lie back and think of England, or whatever."

I heard Max groan softly and decided that was our cue to exit stage left. I tapped Ron and moved slowly away, staying in a crouch to keep our silhouette from appearing in the front windows. I edged along the wall to the door, then put my hand back until I felt Ron's head bump into it. Then I gently opened the door a crack and got my fingers around the frame. There was going to be no quiet escape. The bell hanging above the door would ensure that. I was just banking on it taking Stubbs a good while to get up and going from his current position. I pulled the door open and the light outside flooded in; the bell rang out, sounding like Big Ben now, and I dashed out the door, still in a crouch. As I hit the pavement I stood and sprinted, glancing behind to ensure Ron was there.

I clicked the fob and thanked Lizzy's Lord for small mercies like electronic locks, then I dashed around the car and into the driver's seat. Ron landed in his seat as I turned the key, and both our doors flew open as I hit the gas and reversed away from the liquor store I'd parked in front of, out onto Okeechobee Boulevard. They slammed closed as I accelerated away, under the turnpike. Ron turned and looked over his shoulder.

"Nothing," he said. "He's not out."

"That was close," I said, slowing a little as the surge of adrenaline eased.

Ron turned back and sat down. "That was worse than seeing it happen. My mind filled in all the blanks." He shuddered.

"Tell me about it. I'm not going to sleep for a month."

"At least we got something," he said.

"Yeah. Now we just have to find a recording engineer who moonlights."

CHAPTER THIRTY

They say in the last two minutes of a football match, the coach can do nothing but watch. He can pull all the fancy timeouts he wants, but ultimately he has to trust in his players, in their training and their knowledge and their skills. I didn't have many ideas on how to find our mysterious recording engineer, so the next morning I threw the task at Lizzy, and within twenty minutes I had a name, a phone number and an address.

"You're sure it's the guy?"

Lizzy shot me a look that would frighten the socks off Beelzebub himself. "No, I don't know it's the guy. I know it's a guy called Dexter who works as a recording engineer in Miami. That's all I can tell you, because that's all you told me."

"Well, good work," I said.

"Thank you," she said, storming back to her desk.

We made a stop on the way, a quick detour to the auto repair shop where the Escape was undergoing triage. The guy told me the frame might have a hairline fracture, and they would need to X-ray it to be sure, and then he added that the engine block might be cracked. It sounded like brain damage to me, so I told him to euthanize. I was as sure that the insurance would pay for a new car as I was that my premiums were going to end up in the *Guinness Book of Records*. We left and headed down I-95, the traffic building in Lauderdale until it became slow near the airport, and we crept into Miami. The studio we wanted was in a nondescript office building near the water, conveniently just across from Star Island, where plenty of recording artists had winter homes. The lobby was plastered with gold and platinum records in frames and posters for albums that had been recorded there. I didn't recognize half of them. There was plenty of hip-hop looking stuff, plus the Bee Gees and the Miami Sound Machine. The receptionist was bottle blond, wore shocking pink lipstick and looked about twelve years old, but was kind enough to call Dexter when I said I was from Max Stubbs Management and I had met Dexter at an industry party.

Dexter looked like a stuntman, or a bouncer at a nightclub. He was about six three, heavy without having gone completely to flab, and he wore a trendy, close-cropped beard. His shirt looked like the Tommy Bahama palm print I was wearing, but turned out to be microphones and skulls, whatever that was supposed to mean. He frowned as I put my hand out.

"Come inside," he said, without shaking hands.

We followed him along a hallway lined with more records and photos of Ricky Martin and Enrique Iglesias and a bunch of other nameless faces into a recording studio. Once the door closed it was so quiet it was like the outside world ceased to exist.

"You guys work for Max?" said Dexter.

"More or less," I said.

"I told him to never come here. It's not cool, man."

"I know, I know," I said. "You don't want your moonlighting work to interfere with your professional life."

"You better believe it, and you better leave now."

"Before we do, I just wanted to ask about the edits you did for him. The meeting with a guy called Julio."

Dexter frowned. "You want to know what?"

"What happened to the original files?"

Dexter looked at me in my Tommy B and chinos, then at Ron in his Nautica shirt and Helly Hansen trousers, and his frown grew. "You guys don't work for Stubbs."

"What makes you say that?" I said.

"You're too well dressed, for starters."

I nodded. The guy knew classy threads when he saw them.

"You got us," I said. "We don't work for Stubbs. We work for the guy he's trying to frame."

"Get out," said Dexter, pointing at the door of the studio.

"Before you get all feisty—" I said.

"Get. Out!" His throat started to pulse and his face grew red.

I put my palms up, but Ron stepped forward.

"What does he have on you?" said Ron.

"What? Nothing. Now please leave."

Ron shook his head. "Stubbs is not a cool cat," he said, sounding like a Doobie Brother. "He's framing a good guy for something he didn't do, and you're helping. We're going to prove that. Now it's up to you to decide if you go down with Stubbs or if we help you, too."

Dexter looked at us both again but didn't relax. "How can you help me?"

"He's got something on you, hasn't he? Just like he has on our friend," said Ron.

Dexter took a deep breath. He was on the edge, between a rock and a whole world of hurt, to mix a metaphor. He was trying to decide if he could trust us, if we were the lesser of two evils. I was going to prod him along, but sometimes the best thing to do to gain someone's trust is to simply keep your trap shut. Dexter got there himself. He stepped around some microphone stands, over to a sofa in the corner of the studio, and flopped down.

"He has pictures of me," said Dexter.

"Okay," I said.

"Pictures of me with a woman," he said.

"All right, well that's not the end of the world."

He looked at me. His frown had been replaced by a look of . . . was it fear? No, it was the look of a small boy, who had done something that was going to disappoint Mom in a very big way.

"I don't think my wife would agree," he said.

"Oh," I said.

"It was foolish. Just the one time. Well, just those few times. She was an artist, and . . . Well . . . you know. But it was a year ago, and I haven't done anything like that since and I never will again."

I wasn't a priest and I wasn't a psychologist, but with this dude on the sofa, I kind of got a feeling for the job. "Dexter. Can I call you Dexter?" I said. "I get it. You made a mistake, and this guy is blackmailing you. I tell you what. You help us out, we'll find those pictures for you. Your wife never has to know."

Dexter took a big gulp and a deep breath. "How will you get them?" he asked. "I don't know where they are."

"Don't worry about that. We found you, didn't we? We know what we're doing. We can find your pictures. And take Stubbs down in the process."

A small smile edged its way onto Dexter's mouth. He nodded. "Okay, one minute."

He stood and left the studio, and for a moment I thought he might have done a runner, but he returned in a few minutes and handed me a CD.

"I burned this," he said. "It has all the original files from Stubbs's recording device."

"How did you do it?" I said.

"Easy. He got audio of the guy talking, saying things in a completely different context. Like he'd ask the guy 'Can you throw that ball at a hundred miles an hour?' and the guy would answer 'Of course I can do that,' then I splice a recording of Stubbs saying something like 'Can you fix this game?' and edit it in with the guy's other answer, and voila, a whole different conversation."

"It sounds authentic," I said.

"Of course. I'm good at what I do. You think half the singers who come in here actually sound that good? Hell, no. A few even use my dubs in their live shows."

"But wouldn't someone be able to tell?" said Ron. "Aren't there ways?"

"Of course, if you were an expert and analyzed the wave patterns. I told Stubbs that. I said it would never pass a challenge in court. But he said it didn't matter."

"Of course not. He wasn't planning on going anywhere near a courtroom," I said.

"Which reminds me," said Dexter. "This won't be going near a court. You do that, I'll deny everything, and I know how to get rid of all the evidence so even a forensic analyst won't find it."

"No, Dexter. We're not going anywhere near a court, either."

Dexter walked us out, and I said we wouldn't be in touch and he said that was good. We got back into the car and I tossed the CD to Ron.

"Okay," I said, starting the car. "So we know Stubbs was framing Julio. The question remains, who put him up to it?"

"Whoever was sending the death threats," said Ron.

"That's my guess," I said.

"Which sort of puts us back at square one."

"Not exactly," I said. "Now we have a link between Julio and whoever is threatening the pelotari. Stubbs."

Ron nodded. "And some ammunition to use against him," he said, holding up the disk.

"Exactly."

I pulled out and headed back toward the freeway.

"But that leaves one thing. How do we get the photos back from Stubbs? The ones of Dexter."

"We don't," I said.

"Huh, not like you to leave a guy hanging like that," said Ron.

"You see the receptionist at that studio?"

"Pretty girl. Your point?"

"Bright pink lipstick. The same color lipstick that was on Dexter's collar. Either he hasn't done laundry in a year or he's a lying, cheating sack of manure."

CHAPTER THIRTY—ONE

We got back to West Palm for a late lunch and decided to hit up Longboard's. Mick was boiling peel and eats that Muriel said had come from a friend's boat in the gulf. Gulf shrimp are pink to begin with and sweet, and we nodded an emphatic *yes* at the idea. Despite the cloud cover and cool breeze, Muriel was still in her tank top, little goosebumps forming on her arms. Somewhere in the inside bar came the patter of golf claps from the television.

"So you think we should just spring it on him?" said Ron, taking a long pull on his beer.

I didn't touch mine. I was deep in thought, but not about Max Stubbs. Ron's comment pulled me back.

"Hmm? Oh, Stubbs. I don't know. I sure would like to see the look on his face when we did spring it on him."

"But then he'd know it was us running out the door of his office."

"Pretty sure he's going to figure that out sooner or later, anyway," I said. "My bigger concern is what he does when he learns about it. If we don't know who hired him, he might take it to them, and that makes our job much harder."

"True enough. But if we don't use him, then we aren't any closer, are we?" he said, sipping.

"I'm not saying we don't use him. It's like having a killer play in football, one you know is going to bamboozle the opposition. You don't pull it out in the preseason. You wait until it's really going to count."

"Okay, so . . ."

I sipped my beer then held the bottle up. "We know Stubbs was setting up Julio, and that he wasn't doing that off his own bat. Someone got him to do it. And we know that that someone also threatened Julio—and Perez for that matter."

"Agreed. So?"

"So there are two ends to the thread. Stubbs at one end, the threats at the other. The same person is pulling the strings. If we can't pull one end loose yet, maybe we can pull the other."

"Are you thinking out loud? 'Cause you're losing me," said Ron.

"A trap. We set a trap."

Ron nodded and thought it through. As he did, a group came in through the courtyard entrance and took up position under a faded umbrella. They were ladies just come from tennis, and once upon a time would have been ripe for the picking for Ron. I glanced at him and saw him watching them sit. He smiled to himself—something that looked sneakily like contentment—then spun back around on his stool and faced the bar.

We ate delicious shrimp with a side of fries and then made our way back to the office. Lizzy was out at the post office, doing I had no idea what, so we went into my office and made calls. I had a plan, and we needed to prepare in order to put it into action. I called Julio to tell him to hang in there, that I had proof he didn't do anything wrong, then I called Miami marina and left a message. Ron wandered down to the local print shop to get some artwork made up and some flyers printed. The print shop told him it would take an hour to turn the job around, which seemed lightning fast to me but didn't impress Lizzy at all.

"You should leave that stuff to me," she said.

"You weren't here," I replied.

"You should just leave it to me."

There was no arguing with that logic. Once Ron returned from the print shop we headed over to the fronton. Roto had gathered all the pelotari, at my request. Their performance tonight was in the evening, so they had come early to help out. We hit the streets, around the fronton mainly, but then down around the airport and up A1A toward downtown West Palm, and we handed out flyers to anyone we saw. We taped them to light poles, posted them in storefront windows, tacked them on notice boards in the grocery. As a team, we plastered the area with paper promoting the fronton and the following week's mega championship series.

There was no championship series. I'd made it up.

I could have been a promoter like Don King, except without the crazy hair. The idea had come to me at Longboard's, when I heard the golf on the television. Golf has no season; it runs more or less all year, depending on where the weather is good. But this means outside of the majors, there is no season winner, no champion. So they created one. Out of thin air, they just decided that the tournaments in the latter part of the US season would become playoffs, and at the end there would be a champion. It was forced, fake and fooled almost no one, but it gave golf fans and ESPN and the Golf Channel something to try to give a damn about. So I copied them and created the Jai Alai Championship Series. The best against the best. The fact it was the same guys anyone could see week in, week out at the fronton was beside the point. It would generate interest, and it would generate publicity.

And it would come to the attention of whoever was sending the threats.

After we had gotten rid of most of the flyers, we met back at the fronton. I had outlined the plan to Roto, who wasn't that keen at first but warmed to it once I told him to send his family to Orlando for the weekend. The pelotari left to get ready for their performance, and Ron and I adjourned to the bar in the casino. I left a flyer with the bartender, who smiled and shook his head, then brought us drinks. I put some money down on the bar, but the bartender waved it away.

"Comped," he said.

"Why?" I asked.

He shrugged. "Ms. Almondson says so."

Ron made his impressed face, and we clinked glasses. College football was on the television, University of Florida and some non-conference team they were going to murder, so I lost interest. Ron swiveled around to watch. I tore at a paper napkin and thought about what I was doing. It was a hunch, a ploy to drive whoever was behind all this bad stuff out from under their rock. I had been confident in the plan, happy we had covered the bases, that the best people were in place, and that we were ready if, or when, it went pear-shaped in some way.

But now, sitting in the dark bar, I couldn't get my mind off Danielle. I had taken a similar risk before, beating the bushes to drive the bad guys out, thinking I was only risking myself. But Danielle had been caught in the middle. The bad guys had gone after her instead, on my blindside, and she had been shot and nearly killed. It weighed heavily on me, despite her constant reassurance that I wasn't responsible. Since then, she had moved in with me—we said out of convenience, but I knew part of me wanted her close to protect her. Protect a law enforcement officer who could subdue a suspect twice her weight in a dozen different ways, and needed protecting like I needed to learn how to throw a curve ball. And since then, things had been good. Comfortable.

We had fallen into a nice routine, spending time on the patio in the evenings she didn't work, me taking fewer cases so I was there when she got home. We ran on the beach, not as regularly as we had, but enough, and we made love more than most. It was nice. It was comfortable. It was the home life I'd never had as a kid. And it was the reason I felt like I was losing her.

Ron spun around on his stool and banged his glass down. "Time?"

I nodded and left my beer, and we wandered back through the gaming floor to the fronton. A small crowd had gathered, maybe fifty people. Although the champion series was the following week, clearly our marketing blitz had brought in a few extras. Prior to the performance, Roto took the microphone from the zealous announcer and stood before the audience.

"Ladies and gentlemen," he said, taking a gulp and looking my way with a sheepish frown. I nodded and gestured to keep going.

"Thank you for coming to tonight's performance. As you may know, next week we will see our champions series, the best of jai alai in the world."

The crowd gave a little applause, nothing to give you goose bumps, but something at least. Roto paused and looked to me again. I could see him sweating across his brow, his athletic frame seeming to shrink as he stood in the spotlight. English wasn't his first language, so that accounted for some of the nerves. But this was the important part of the night, and I smiled as reassuringly as I could and nodded him on.

"My name is Roto. I am one of the pelotari, the players of jai alai, and I am responsible for promoting this event."

There it was, and if the sniper's crosshairs weren't on him now, they never would be.

"I hope you join us for the championship series, and please tell your friends and family. We look forward to seeing the jai alai of old, here in West Palm next week."

Another smattering of applause and Ron and I moved across the seating, handing out the last of the flyers. Roto had done well, had sold the thing even better than I'd hoped. But he had put himself in danger. The first two pelotari took the court and began play. Roto took his place on the bench and looked my way again. I gave him the thumbs up, and he gave me a tight smile, then turned and focused on the game.

After play, Roto showered and changed, then came back out to the fronton court and led me across the seating area to a rear door. We crept out the back, and I found myself on the gravel, where Lucas and I had our first run in with the Boston Irishmen. My rental car was waiting in the shadows just around the corner, where Ron had left it. Roto got in the backseat and lay down, then I pulled out and flashed my lights at Ron, who was sitting in Roto's car. I pulled out south, to head down around the airport, then cut back up north to my place. Ron turned the other way, onto the island where he would hide Roto's car in the secure lot below Cassandra's apartment. If anyone went to do anything at Roto's house tonight, they would find no one home, and anyone waiting for Roto in the shadows would have no idea where he had disappeared. I had thought about setting the trap tonight, but the kid at the marina told me Lucas wouldn't be back from his boat delivery until the following day, and I needed him. Plus, I couldn't be sure the bad guys would pick up the scent so fast. However, after the performance and the crowd the flyers had brought in, I doubted that. But it was fine to let them think on it a bit. When we offered the bait up for the taking, they would be all the more hungry.

CHAPTER THIRTY—TWO

The next day was Saturday, and with Roto's family confirmed safe in a hotel at Disney World, we spent the day waiting. Julio wanted to come over, but we couldn't be sure he wasn't being followed, so we nixed the idea. Having slept fitfully in my spare room, Roto wore dark circles under his eyes at breakfast. I could see he was getting the jitters just sitting around waiting for the evening performance to come, so I decided to take a field trip.

I had received a call from my insurance agent to let me know that they had written off the SUV for insurance purposes, and I was free to replace the vehicle with something of equal value. She left me with the afterthought that as this was the third car they had replaced on my behalf, I had been reclassified as a high-risk client. I smiled at the thought, and wondered what kind of coverage Dale Earnhardt Jr. had.

Roto and I wandered along the dealerships at the nice end of Okeechobee Boulevard. Roto was quite the family man and conservative to boot, and he smiled and nodded at every minivan we went near. I had gone from a convertible Mustang to a hybrid Escape, and I wasn't ready to drop into a minivan—as much as Ron would have laughed himself hoarse at the idea. We lingered a little too long at the Lamborghini dealership and skipped the Volvo place altogether. We took a used Porsche Boxster for a spin, and with the top down and the breeze whipping through my hair, I started to see myself in it. Roto wasn't so impressed.

"It is only two doors," he said.

"So?" I frowned.

"What happens when you want to have *los bebes*?"

I had nothing to say to that, so I walked away. In the end we occupied ourselves at CityPlace, where we wandered the mall, window-shopping, and I replaced my water-damaged phone.

By the time we were ready to head to the fronton, Roto's hands were shaking so much I didn't think he would be able to put on his cesta. We got in the rental car and headed down A1A, checking my mirrors but seeing no one. Ron was en route from Palm Beach in Roto's car, and Lucas had returned and was on board, heading north up I-95 as we moved south to the casino. I pulled into the lot and saw Ron standing by Roto's ride, a very plain-looking sedan that he promised got excellent mileage, and I stopped right beside. Ron went in first, then Roto, and I

took the rear. There was no one watching us, nothing
suspicious to see, and Roto went and got changed for the
performance without incident. Once inside, I was fairly
confident nothing would happen. There was too much
security now that Jenny had beefed it up, and outside the
locker rooms there were cameras everywhere. Besides, the
flyers had actually done something and the crowd was
over a hundred strong. Even a news crew from the local
affiliate had turned up.

Ron and I drank iced tea as we watched the
performance, but we didn't eat. I could tell he was as
nervous as I was—and not just for Roto. We were all
putting ourselves out now, and although it certainly made
me feel alive, there was a twisted gut to go along with it.
Roto managed to get his big woven basket on his hand,
but he shouldn't have bothered. Not surprisingly, he got
slaughtered and didn't take a point all night. All the other
pelotari had a rough idea of what was happening, and
they played easy against him, but Roto was a mess, and I
realized without the proper technique how dangerous the
pelota could be, flung in the random fashion it was
coming out of Roto's cesta.

The performance finished, and the crowd shuffled
out onto the gaming floor. Roto and the others showered,
and Ron and I waited in our seats.

"You ready for this?" he said.

I nodded. "As ready as ever."

"You're the one who will be in danger."

"Thanks, Ron. Appreciate the heads-up."

"Sorry. Just be careful."

"Let's all be careful."

Roto drove his own car. This time it was my turn to lie on the backseat as he headed home to his townhouse. Ron was in my rental car, not tailing us but heading in the same general direction. Lucas was already in place, in a sniper's perch on top of the apartment block opposite Roto's townhouse. As we headed out west to Roto's home, I called Lucas.

"This is Lucas," he whispered.

"How's it look?"

"All quiet."

"You sure about this?" I asked. "You don't have to do this. It's not your war anymore."

"It's always my war, mate. It's just whether I get involved that changes. Besides, this is just keeping my eye in."

"All right. If you're sure. We're about ten minutes out," I whispered back, though I didn't know why.

"Roger that."

Roto told me when we were approaching, and he hit the clicker to open his garage door. I saw the white walls of the garage through the windows and heard the chain grind the door closed. I sat up. Once inside, I made sure all the drapes were pulled and the lights were on. I had Roto put on some music, and he chose mariachi, which I thought was a bit obvious, so he changed to some Gloria Estefan.

"Okay, you can sit here in the living room until we hear from Ron or Lucas," I said. "Then I'll want you to move as we discussed. Okay?"

"Si."

"And stay away from the windows."

"Si."

We waited through an entire Gloria Estefan album, then a Miami Sound Machine greatest hits, then Roto dropped in some Spanish guitar, which hit the spot. I hadn't expected company immediately upon getting there, but by two in the morning I was flagging. I hoped the other guys were okay. I called Ron, and he was awake, if not alert. We agreed there was a chance that no one would show tonight. Perhaps they would bide their time, and we'd have to do this again. I wasn't sure how we would sell the idea to Roto's wife, who thought the Disney trip was something that Roto had won but couldn't take with them due to his in-season playing commitments. My phone vibrated in my hand to kill that thought.

"This is Lucas."

"You know," I said. "Shouldn't we have code names or something?"

"We do. Mine's Lucas. I thought you'd like to know there are two big dudes with guns approaching the townhouse."

I turned and shot a look at Roto, who needed no further information.

"Where's your guy?" said Lucas.

"He's getting in the bathtub with a bottle of tequila."

"Good plan. Stay open channels. Bogies one house away."

I slipped the phone into my pocket and slipped the attached earphone into one ear. Then I reached into the back of my jeans and pulled out my Glock. I had felt it against my back all night, like a spider sleeping on my skin. Despite my body heat it hadn't warmed up, and I looked at it like it was death itself. It was heavy for its size, like a good watermelon, but unlike a watermelon, its purpose had nothing to do with warm summer afternoons and happy times. I had the thing because Lenny demanded I have it just in case, demanded I spend hours at the range learning to use it, and then the first time I'd ever fired it outside the range, I had killed the man who had killed Lenny. Lenny, like Lucas, had been much more at ease with weapons, as if they were hammers or saws. I spoke to Lucas as I moved back from the window, imagining him looking through the scope on his sniper's rifle.

"News?" I said.

"Just the two guys. Now, we need to make sure of that fact, so I'm going to hold my powder until the last. You keep ya pants on, ya hear?"

"Roger that."

I pulled the chamber back on the Glock to arm it and got behind the side of the sofa. I hoped I wouldn't have to use it, but I wouldn't hesitate if I had to. Lenny had drummed that much into me. *Don't pick it up unless you're prepared to use it. Don't aim it at anything you ain't prepared to shoot. Shoot so whatever you aim at ain't getting up again.*

"Okay, we've got two guys," said Lucas through my earpiece. "One is at the window, the other approaching the door. The window guy has a shotgun, the door guy I can't tell, but probably a handgun from his stance."

"You're sure there's no way in through the back?" I whispered, despite the fact that the music was blaring.

"No, mate. I had a good look when I got here. No access from the back. Personally, I'd come in from above, but I don't think these fellas have chopper support. Just hang on a sec, got another call coming in."

I rolled my eyes at Lucas taking another call right now. It was like taking a call during your wedding ceremony. Then he was back.

"That was Ron," he said. "He thought he saw one of the guys from his spot. He's got good eyes."

"Anything coming from his way?"

"Nada," said Lucas. "This is it. These are our guys. Hang tight."

There was nothing but silence on the line. The Spanish guitar bounced into my brain and back out again. I felt like my whole body was shaking, but I looked down at the gun and found my hand to be as steady as a surgeon's. Then Lucas was back.

"Okay, they're down. Wait ten seconds."

I waited what felt like hours.

"Okie dokes, we're good. I'll see you out front," said Lucas. He clicked off the call. I didn't get up immediately.

The whole thing felt like an anticlimax, and I waited for the extra guy to spring out of the darkness, but he didn't. I got up and, holding the Glock with two hands, I made my way to the front door. I took one hand off the gun to unlock and open the door, then I threw it open and pushed myself up against the jamb. But there was nothing out there. Then I saw the first guy. He was lying at my feet, on the path to the door. I craned my head around to look back toward the living room window and saw the second guy. He had fallen into the plants at the base of the window. I stepped out and looked at both guys. They looked dark, but it was the wee hours and hard to tell. They both wore sleeveless shirts, and they both had long black hair, tied back in a sort of ponytail. I thought of what Roto's cousin had seen. Two Indians with long hair. These guys fit the bill. Sort of. The more I looked, the more things didn't feel right. I knew plenty of muscular Seminole, and these guys didn't look like that. They were heavier somehow, and the hair seemed to burst from where it was tied back, rather than fall down their backs.

"How ya doing?" said Lucas, and I looked up to see him wandering across the road with two rifle bags in his hands. He dropped the bags on the lawn, then approached the two bodies.

"First things first," he said. "Let's get any weapons." He grabbed the shotgun from the flowerbed, and I picked up a six-shooter from the guy on the doorstep.

"Should we have gloves on?" I said.

Lucas shook his head. "Nah, doesn't matter, not where these guns are gonna end up."

He took the gun from me and put them with his rifles.

"You sure about this stuff?" I said.

"Oh yeah, dead set. Pinched it from a fella who was gonna shoot little sharks for fun. I mean, if sharks don't swim, they drown. Even for a shark, that don't seem very sporting."

He leaned over the guy in the garden and pulled out a huge tranquilizer dart. It looked big enough to down a hippo. Lucas came over to the guy at the door.

"This fella spun when I hit him, so he's probably got the dart under him."

Lucas bent down and rolled the guy over. Then he stood up and gave me a frown.

"Thought you said these fellas were Seminoles?"

"That was the information I got," I said.

"Well, this fella's no Seminole."

"I can see that. What is he?"

"See that tattoo there on his arm," said Lucas. "I know that tattoo. This guy is Tongan."

CHAPTER THIRTY—THREE

The warehouse was a massive space on the Loxahatchee River that had once been used to house luxury boats under repair, according to Lucas. Now it was empty, the floors littered with papers and rodent droppings. I didn't exactly get Lucas's method, but he was in a mood that was hearing no arguments. There was a job to be done, and he was going to do it.

With more effort than it should have taken three men, we had pulled each of the tranquilized Tongans into the back of Lucas's pickup, then Ron and I followed him to the warehouse. I for one was glad Lucas didn't get pulled over on the way. His cargo would have been hard to explain. But we'd gotten there without incident, and it had taken the three of us to unload our human cargo and place them where they now sat.

Lucas said he had used a quarter-dose tranquilizer, maybe good for an hour of downtime. Where he got his data, I had no idea. The first Tongan started to wake with several hard slaps to the face.

"Wakey, wakey," said Lucas with a smile.

The Tongan didn't share the emotion. The instant he started to zero in on his situation, he tried to move, but was stopped by the fact he had been hog-tied to a post. He was just as immobile awake as he had been unconscious, but he struggled anyway. His movement roused his partner from his slumber, and he repeated the process, the two of them struggling with all their might, back to back, tied to a pole by a guy who could have held the *Titanic* together with rope.

"Okay, boys, when you're done, we'll chat," said Lucas.

The Tongans must have figured they had fully tested the quality of the bindings, because they settled and glared at Lucas.

"Right, better. So here's the sitrep. You fellas turned up tonight, planning to kill a friend of ours. In our books, that's uncool. So we want to know who sent you."

One of the Tongans spat, and the other gave a throaty, mirthless laugh.

"Now," continued Lucas, "obviously I don't expect you fellas to give out that kind of information without an incentive. So I'm going to provide you with one. We could play games all night, drag it out of you slow, but

I've got to be at work in a couple hours, so I don't really have that luxury."

Lucas paced around in a half circle, and the Tongans' heads flipped around to follow.

"I tell you this so you understand my predicament, so you get what I'm doing. Because right now, you think that my timeline gives you the advantage. You think if I have to leave, you just have to hold out for a little while. Please let me dissuade you of that notion."

Lucas crouched on his haunches and got in close to the big guys.

"Worst case, boys? You hold out and I leave. But I leave you here for a day or two. No water; no way out. Then I come back and finish the job. So you see how you don't have an advantage at all? Your choices are limited to two. Tell me what I need to know, or get nice and comfy with a mother lode of pain."

He smiled and stood slowly, then turned to Ron and I and winked. I'd seen Lenny do some pretty crazy stuff, but Lucas made Lenny look like the sanest person in the world. Ron leaned into me.

"You sure he knows what he's doing?" he said.

I shook my head. "I'm sure there's no stopping him. Beyond that, I know nothing."

Lucas turned his attention to the Tongans. "I served with a few fellas from Tonga, you know. Played rugby with a lot of 'em, too. Big guys, tough in the tackle, but nice fellas, to a man. You boys really give your people a bad name, you know that?"

"You're no advert for Aussie, bro," said one of the Tongans.

Lucas smiled. "So, he talks."

"Not to you, bro. Not telling you nothing. So do your worst."

Lucas looked at his watch, then at the Tongans. "You're right. Best get on with it."

He took a Zippo lighter from his pocket and flicked the flame on. "You fellas notice what you're sitting on? That's a lot of newspaper. And that lumpy stuff you can feel underneath? Those are what we grill masters like to call fire starters."

Lucas crouched between the two Tongans and held the Zippo to the paper. It began burning, curling in on itself, more intent on putting itself out than spreading the flame. Lucas lit a couple more spots, then moved to the other side of the pole and repeated the process. I watched the first spot fire, almost out, the edge of the paper glowing orange but curling black. Then the orange touched a fire starter, and for a moment there was nothing. No orange, no flame, no smoke—like the whole thing had gone out. *The quiet before the storm* was the cliché that bounced into my mind. Then the fire starter flickered and caught, and flames leaped upward and joined the spots next to them, where the other fire starters began catching and joining in the burn.

It took a moment, but the Tongans caught on eventually. Before any flame touched them they tried wriggling out of their binds once more, and when that failed they tried blowing the flames out. It wasn't a bonfire, but I figured it was enough to create the sensation of being barbecued alive.

"You crazy, bro," said one of the Tongans. I noted the beginnings of fear in his eyes as the flames lapped at his sleeveless arms.

"Talk to me, mate," said Lucas. "Who sent you?"

"No way," said the Tongan.

"Burn, baby, burn," said Lucas, and he edged around the pyre to the other Tongan. "How 'bout you, mate?" he said.

The flames were lapping higher under this guy, and the side of his shirt caught fire. He was breathing heavy and panicking, and when flame burst up between his legs, he lost it.

"Okay, bro. Our cousin sent us. Our cousin," he said, trying to blow out the flames lapping at his groin.

"Who is your cousin?" said Lucas, as relaxed as a picnicker.

"Finau, his name is Finau."

Lucas looked up at me. "That name mean something to you?" he asked.

It did. I moved to the other Tongan, the not-so-chatty one, whose jeans were starting to smolder.

"That true?" I said. "Is Finau your cousin, too?"

"Yeah, bro, yeah," he said, suddenly getting more cooperative.

"Why does Finau want to hurt the jai alai players?" I asked.

"He don't, man. He don't. It's a scare. Bro, I'm burning up here."

"Then talk quick," I said. "Why is he doing this?"

"It's not our cousin, it's that lady. The lady he works for."

"Jenny Almondson?"

"Yeah, that's the one. She's doing it. She tells Finau what to do. He says she wants us to dress up like Indians and shake down some guys. That's all I know. Bro, I'm on fire!"

And he was. The hairs across his arms glowed like a thousand cigars, and the skin had started to char. I looked at Lucas and nodded, then he wandered casually over to his truck and pulled out an extinguisher, which he used to douse both the flames and the Tongans. Once the area was a sea of foam, we convened at the bed of his truck.

"Who is this Jenny sheila?" said Lucas.

"She runs the Jai Alai and Casino," I said.

"Everything goes back to that casino," said Lucas. "Desi, those Boston dudes, this. That place is rancid."

"Rotten to the core," I said.

"All right, well I gotta get to work," said Lucas. "You fellas okay?"

"What about these guys?"

Lucas seemed to have forgotten the Tongans already. He turned to them.

"Now, boys, we're gonna go, and you're gonna stay here. I want you to think on your sins for a little while, get me? You should be doing your ancestors proud, not carrying on like this."

"You can't leave us, bro. I got burns."

"Think of it like a tattoo," said Lucas. "A reminder of poor choices made. We'll call your people in a little while, tell them where you are."

He turned back to me and fished his keys from his pocket. "Wait until you decide what you wanna do with the casino thing, then call and tell them where these two are."

He walked to the cab of his truck and got in.

"Just try to do it before they start going septic, yeah?" he said. Then he fired up the truck and pulled out.

Ron and I walked out into the cool night, the dawn still an hour from joining us.

"That was different," said Ron.

"You could say."

"Where do you think he learned that?"

"I don't want to know," I said.

And I didn't. I wasn't sure what things Lucas had seen in his life, but I feared a lot of them were not good. I shuddered at the thought of what Danielle would say about what we had done. We got to the rental car, and Ron looked across the roof at me.

"They weren't just going to scare Roto tonight. They were going to kill him," he said.

I nodded.

"It's gone way beyond scaring," I said. "Which means they're panicking. But the question is, why?"

CHAPTER THIRTY—FOUR

I was sitting on the patio with an orange-berry smoothie, watching the sunrise reflect off the windows in Riviera Beach, when my phone rang. I looked at the screen and saw it was Danielle.

"Morning," I said.

"Hey, you. I didn't wake you did I?"

"Nah, I'm on the patio. Couldn't sleep."

"What's up?" she said.

"I think we've figured out who has been threatening the jai alai guys." I figured I'd leave out how we had come about that discovery.

"That's great," she said. "Case closed?"

"Not quite. There's a little question of why."

"Are the jai alai players paying you to find out why?" she said.

It was a good point. I had been engaged to find out who was making the threats. I wasn't on the payroll to figure out their motives. But once I started digging a hole, I really wanted to know if there was oil down there.

"It's sort of implied that we try to stop it happening, and at the moment I don't have enough to take to court."

"Well, I'm glad you are considering involving the proper authorities." I could hear the teasing in her voice.

"Wherever possible, my darling. You know me."

"Yeah, I do," she said, laughing. It was a great sound, one that didn't fit with the rest of my night, but one that brought a smile to my face nevertheless.

"So what about you? You're up early. How's the conference."

"It was great. An eye-opener."

"Was great? It's over?"

"Yes, it finished Friday night. But the Atlanta PD and the local FBI field office are doing site visits over the weekend, so the boss thought it was worth me staying. Is that okay?"

"Sure, I guess. I miss you, is all."

"I miss you, too. I'll be back tomorrow at some point, although I might need to go straight into the office."

"You're even starting to sound like a police chief or something," I said.

"I've got to tell you, MJ, I've learned a lot. You hear so much about all this interdepartmental jealousy, jurisdictional lines, and all that. But there was none of that. Everyone is trying to help everyone else do a better job of keeping the streets safe. I was excited by all the cooperative efforts that departments were putting in place. I've even got a few ideas to bring home. Hopefully the boss will let me implement some."

"He'd be a fool not to."

"Thanks, MJ. You know, I also learned a lot about me, too. The chiefs and sheriffs I met all have one thing in common. They don't sit around waiting for things to happen. I need to be like that, I think, if I want to be one of them."

"You are one of them. I've seen the uniform."

"But you know what I mean."

"I do."

And I did. She was growing. A little bit of water and she had sprouted like the first summer tomatoes.

"You just can't sit still in law enforcement," she said. "There's no place for complacency. If you're not moving forward, then you are going backward. I feel like I might have been guilty of that lately, you know what I mean?"

Again, I did. I just wasn't sure if she meant professionally or in her life with me, too. Comfortable for one person is complacent for another. I wondered if I had been drifting in happiness, using it as an excuse for not moving forward. When I'd played baseball I always had forward momentum. I was always trying to be better, fitter. To get into the next team, or up into the next league. It drove me, all the way to the majors. And when Oakland let me go, it still drove me, because I had had a taste, and the Mets offered a lifeline. And then, suddenly, one day the desire to keep improving, to keep moving forward was gone. And at the end of that season I hung up my cleats. I wondered if I was losing my drive again. And if I was, what had I been after, anyway? To be a better PI? A better friend? A better partner? Had I kept myself in shape so I could find Danielle, and now that I had her, let the drive in me die away? A guy didn't stay in the major league by coasting.

"I think you can be anything you want to be," I said.

"Right back at ya," she said. "But you know what else I learned this week? Teamwork is everything."

I nodded even though she couldn't see me. That was also true in baseball. I hadn't realized how true it was everywhere else. My mind played through the faces on my team: Danielle, Ron, Lucas. Cassandra, Lenny, Sally Mondavi, Lizzy, Mick. Danielle again. The idea of teamwork stuck in my mind like a burr. And that competitors were not always exactly that. What it meant I wasn't sure yet, but I knew from experience that those kinds of mental burrs stuck for a reason.

"You're a very smart woman, you know that?" I said.

"Someone has to keep the ledger even with you," she giggled. "Listen, I have to get going. I'll see you tomorrow. I love you."

"And I you."

I put the phone down and looked over the Intracoastal. The cloud cover had eased and the water sparkled like a jewel. I turned to look at the empty lounger beside me, and I suddenly couldn't wait for tomorrow to come. But first, I had to get through today. And that wasn't going to happen without some sleep. I leaned back and closed my eyes, looking for rest but finding only Jenny Almondson.

I still found it hard to believe she was behind the death threats. I liked her. She was smart and self-assured, and all business when business was called for. Thugs and threats just didn't suit her. I had to concede that my judgment could be faulty when it came to pretty women, but that notwithstanding, there was still that big question hanging in the air. Why? Why would Jenny want jai alai to fail? It was a necessary part of her business, one that the state showed no desire to change. If there was no jai alai, there was no casino. They were symbiotic—one could not exist without the other, at least as long as the law said so. I thought about Jenny, in her New York suits, the face of a New York gaming organization. Images floated through my mind, and a figure appeared from the earlier montage of faces, providing me with a way forward. With momentum. I saw Sally Mondavi's face again. I had sought out Eric Edwards's view of the arrangement, but I needed to see it from the other perspective. From a New York point of view. I needed to pay a visit to Sally. And with that momentum in place, I drifted off.

CHAPTER THIRTY-FIVE

Sally Mondavi's Pawn and Cash Checking was on Okeechobee Boulevard on the wrong side of the turnpike. I passed Max Stubbs's office to get there, and realized how close it was, and I wondered how much shady stuff was going on along this road.

Sal's store might have sold the flotsam and jetsam of downtrodden life, but it was more a sideline than a career. Sal's main business ran from out the back of the shop and was based on a lifetime of connections. He, like half of Florida, had come from New Jersey. But unlike most transplants, Sal knew every Shylock, hood and made man from Buffalo to the Keys. So if anyone knew anything about a New York gaming company, it was Sal.

After a couple hours sleep, and with renewed purpose that had sprung from somewhere I couldn't pin down, I drove west. I parked the rental car in front of the pawnshop and wandered in. I made a point of wearing a worn New England Patriots T-shirt and khakis, but the girl sitting in the Plexiglas booth near the front of the store wouldn't have cared if I was naked. I didn't recognize her, but there seemed to be a good deal of turnover in that position. I figured sitting in a plastic box cashing checks was close to cruel and unusual punishment, and even asking *would you like fries with that?* would be a big step up.

Sal was leaning on a glass cabinet at the back of the store, looking at something through a one-eyed microscope attached to his glasses. I weaved through the rows of musical instruments and tables of CDs, toward him. He didn't look up from what I now saw was some kind of gemstone.

"You got a nerve wearing that T-shirt in here," he said.

I smiled. "You haven't even looked at me yet."

"I saw you this morning before you even decided to come here."

"How are you, Sal?"

He finally looked up. One eye was gigantic, until he flicked the microscope thing up. He was an old man, hunched by the years and creased by the events of a long life. He brushed a few wisps of hair across his mostly bald head.

"I'm better than you," he said. "You look like something the cat dragged in."

"My mother used to say that."

"And she would have been right if you were wearing that damned Pats T-shirt."

"Back then, chances were I was."

He shook his head. "I can't hold it against you, being brainwashed as a kid like that."

"Because supporting Gang Green just comes naturally."

"On high from God," he said. "This is the Jets' year, I tell you."

"Third place in the division. Looking good."

"Aach, we'll come home strong. You come here just to give an old man a stroke?"

I told him about the casino, about the death threats, about the Tongans telling us Jenny was behind it.

"That Lucas is a screw loose of a picnic," he said. "Gets results, though."

"So what do you think?"

"I know the company, of course. They have some interests in Jersey and here in Florida. Word is they want more action, but authorities are, shall we say, wary of firms with New York family connections."

"There are family connections?"

"There are always connections."

"What about Vegas casinos? Elroy Hoskin is really pushing his project in Palm Beach."

Sally gave a phlegmy laugh. "I'll say Tom Brady is better than Joe Namath before the Palm Beach elites agree to a casino. The Vegas boys might bring big numbers to rival the Seminole, but the best the state can get then is what they get now, but from double the number of casinos. Where's the logic in that?"

"So New York can't get in, and Vegas can't get in. So why is everyone trying so hard? Help me out here, Sal."

Sally scratched his stubble and nodded to himself. "Your girl at the casino might think killing the jai alai strengthens her case," he said. "The logic is that if they can show that the jai alai or ponies are killing jobs or driving the casinos out of business, the state might waive the pari-mutuel requirement. But her logic would be faulty. Not having the sports only helps if they use that space for more gaming, and the state isn't going to approve more gambling sites, and they aren't going to walk away from the Indian money. Game, set, match Seminoles."

"I'm going around in circles here, Sal. I see what you're saying about the Jenny and New York connection, but I don't get why Vegas is getting so heavy if there's no chance of more licenses. Hoskin must know that."

Sally folded his bottom lip over his top, in thought. "When you played ball, you ever have a day where the ball didn't come out so good, but you got out with no runs, anyway?"

"Sure."

"You ever ask yourself why?"

"Nope. That would be tempting the gods."

Sal nodded.

"You're saying I should close the case and take my paycheck."

"Sometimes you don't get to know why."

"That's what Danielle said."

"She's a smart girl. You should hang on to her."

I nodded and thanked Sally for his counsel. He said he had tickets to the Polo fields that he would send me, to take my girl.

"Thanks Sal."

I was going to tell him I owed him one, but he always hated hearing that, so I just wished his football team good luck that afternoon.

"Don't need it," he said, dropping his attention back to the gemstone.

If I knew one thing, it was that Max Stubbs would not work weekends unless a huge wad of cash was waved in front of his pudgy face, so there was no point in hitting up his office on a Sunday. Instead, I headed toward the coast and around Palm Beach International. I drove past the spot where Lucas and I had left the three guys from the bookie's van lying by the side of the road, and on autopilot I cruised around past the casino. I had nothing to do there and didn't plan on showing my face until I had to. I had called the security office from a pay phone at a gas station on Okeechobee Boulevard and left a message for Finau to find his cousins. I knew that was telling them that we knew, but I didn't want those guys developing gangrene or something in their burns. Besides, their failure to return should have told Finau all he needed to know. It was now time to turn the screws.

I slowed by the casino and almost swerved onto the wrong side of the road when I saw the red van parked on the gravel behind the fronton. There were two Mexican-looking guys standing by it. The faces were different, but the play was the same. They shook hands, and everyone climbed into the van and it took off. I pulled off the road, picked up my phone and called, but got voicemail.

"Lucas, I thought you'd want to know. The bookie's van is back in operation at the casino. Catch you soon."

I edged back into traffic and headed to Longboard's for a fish sandwich and a few hours of football. Then it was off home to clean several days worth of dishes in the kitchen so the place didn't look like a barnyard when Danielle got home. Ah, domestic bliss.

CHAPTER THIRTY—SIX

Max Stubbs was also not an early riser, and I had been sitting in the lot for an hour by the time he dragged his carcass into the office. He was pushing open his door when I reached him, so I helped him out and shoved him through. He fell and landed on the worn carpet with a squishy thud. I had brushed his sides as I pushed to confirm he wasn't armed. He rolled over with the grace of a Galapagos tortoise and spluttered at me.

"What the hell?" he said.

I winked.

"You. Who the hell do you think you are? I ought to —"

"Shut up and listen, Stubbs."

He tried to get up and I pushed him back down with my foot.

"I want your full attention," I said. "Here's the deal. I know that it was Jenny Almondson and Finau who hired you to frame Julio."

Stubbs opened his purple lips to protest.

"Don't talk, Stubbs. Just listen. I know all this, so don't waste my time denying it. What I want now is for you to fix it."

Stubbs blinked hard, looking like the animatronic Abraham Lincoln at Disney World. He hesitated, not sure if he should speak.

"You are out of your freakin' mind," were the words he chose.

"Not so, Stubbs. I am perfectly lucid. You, on the other hand, are in deeper doo-doo than the pilgrims in winter."

Stubbs edged up onto his elbows and I let him, but he couldn't support the weight, so he fell back.

"Get up. Sit," I said.

He rolled onto his knees and worked his way into a standing position, then made for his desk.

"No, the sofa," I said. I didn't know if he had a piece in his desk drawer or just bags of Doritos. Either way, he wasn't getting off of that sofa in short order. He flopped down and sank into the worn cushions.

"Stubbs, do you enjoy being a PI?"

He pouted. "It's all right."

"So why do you insist on being so bad at it?"

"Screw you, Jones. You think you're so much better than me."

"Everyone thinks that, Stubbs. But my point is, you're a slob, you're a crook, and you're the reason I can't tell people at parties what I do for a living with a straight face. And now it's time for penance."

"You gonna tie me to a cross?"

"Not without a crane, I'm not. No, you're going to help me make it better."

"Why the hell am I going to do that?"

"Because I know you doctored the audio that was used to frame Julio. I know you got an engineer to create a fake conversation, and you conspired with Mr. Finau and Ms. Almondson to commit fraud."

His jaw dropped lower the more I spoke. By the time I'd finished the thought, he looked like the entrance to the Batcave.

"And if I happen to pass on that audio to the cops, you will definitely lose your PI license, and you'll probably do jail time."

He smacked his lips together several times, like a man walking out of the Sahara. "You can't do this," he said.

"On the contrary, Stubbs. I can."

"I'll never get another client if it gets out that I sold someone out."

"No, you'll never get another crooked client. And being as that is the majority of your client base, I can see how that would be of concern. So you'll just have to drum up more paying Peeping Tom work. After all, man cannot live on blowjobs alone."

He frowned at me, his jaw falling open again as the penny dropped. "You. It was you hiding in my office the other night."

I raised my eyebrows, and Stubbs smiled.

"I'll have you for breaking and entering," he said, way too sure of himself.

"Can't be breaking and entering if nothing is broken."

"Well entering, then," he said, a little less sure.

"Not sure that's actually a charge. Entering? Hmm, no."

"Burglary, that's what it is," he said, pointing at me, like he'd just outsmarted a *Jeopardy* champion.

"Anything missing in your office? No, I didn't think so. Besides, I was at a party in Palm Beach. Lots of people can vouch for me. Lots of important people."

"I didn't say which night it was."

"Doesn't matter, Max. I was at a party. Whatever night."

Max deflated back into the sofa. He'd played his hand and lost. I gave him a minute. He wasn't the brightest spark, but he did have a partially functioning brain, and I wanted him to get there by himself. I watched his cogs ticking over, working the angles, trying to find a loophole. Hope, despair, hope. Then he settled on despair. He looked up at me, forlorn.

"What do I have to do?"

CHAPTER THIRTY—SEVEN

The good news was that I knew Stubbs had all the right equipment. We rigged him up with his secret little microphone, which transmitted the signal to a recorder attached to a hard drive. Apparently the system could email the audio to my Cloud, but I had no idea what that entailed. It was a more sophisticated setup than I'd given Stubbs credit for, but then I saw him in my mind's eyes walking into Best Buy for a tape recorder and getting upsold by a kid with pimples.

Ron and I sat in the car in the lot, just below the window of Jenny Almondson's office, listening to Stubbs huff and puff his way up the elevator. We heard the ding of the elevator, then Finau met him as he got out.

"You shouldn't be here," said Finau.

"We need to talk. About Jones," said Stubbs.

"Not now. I'm on it. He's deader than dead. But you need to lie low."

"I will, right after I speak to Almondson," said Stubbs. He was pretty convincing for a guy who was sweating bullets.

There was nothing but Stubbs's heavy breathing for a while, then the sound of a door opening.

"Hello, Max," said Jenny. Evidently they were in Jenny's office. "What are you doing here?"

"He knows," said Stubbs.

"Who knows what?" she said. She was a cool customer.

"Jones. He knows about the setup. How you, Ms. Almondson, and you, Mr. Finau, set Julio up for illegal betting."

I froze in the car. Stubbs was overdoing it. Getting their names was useful in an audio recording, but no one spoke like that. He was going to get found out.

"Are you all right, Max?"

"I told you, no. He knows."

"He knows what, Max? That you set up Julio for your own reasons and brought fraudulent information to us to ensure you got paid?" said Jenny.

"I did no such thing," said Stubbs.

"That's how it looks, so if I were you, I'd keep quiet," said Jenny.

"It's your people who can't keep quiet," said Stubbs. "They told him what we did."

This must have been directed at Finau, because he replied.

"Settle down, Max. Jones doesn't have any proof we were involved."

"He has the tapes. Aren't you listening?"

"Max, calm down," said Jenny. "What Mr. Jones says can be refuted. You can say that he, not you, doctored the audio so he got paid by Julio."

"No, that won't work," said Stubbs. "The tapes won't pass expert analysis. My guy said so. And you told me this wouldn't go to court. Nowhere near a courthouse, were your exact words, Ms. Almondson."

"Yes, Max, that's right. It isn't going anywhere near a courtroom. We have gotten rid of Julio, and we will make a plan for Mr. Jones."

The audio got louder as I assumed Jenny moved close to Stubbs.

"You just need to keep your pants on, Max."

Suddenly the air was filled with Max's heavy breathing and a muffled groan.

"Can you do that, Max?" said Jenny, all breathy and seductive.

A grunt in the affirmative.

I looked at Ron and he lifted his eyebrows.

"Good boy. My people in New York won't forget you, Max. Nor will Mr. Hoskin."

I spun to look at Ron, and he made his *how the hell would I know* face.

"Now we have work to do, Max. You can see yourself out."

"Sure," said Max. "Sure."

CHAPTER THIRTY-EIGHT

I played the whole thing back again before Stubbs got to the car. That Jenny and Finau were behind things I knew, but the mention of Hoskin had me flummoxed. How did a Vegas competitor have anything to do with them? I transferred a copy of the audio file onto my phone, then got out of the car. Heavy clouds played above and the air smelled wet. Ron and I were leaning on the fenders when Stubbs came around the corner, sweating like a swamp cooler.

"That's it," said Stubbs. He was almost elated, but why I wasn't sure.

"You're done, Stubbs," I said. "You can go."

He frowned. "I don't got a car here. You need to give me a lift."

"Get a cab, Stubbs."

He looked at Ron for support and found none, so he turned back to me. "All right, but now we're equal."

I looked him in the eye. It was my stare-down-the-batter face, and he took a step back.

"We will never, in any way imaginable, be equal. Now get out of my face." It wasn't an act. I really wanted to kick his lardy ass to the gravel.

He took a couple steps back, then looked at Ron.

"I want those tapes back," he said.

Ron nodded and smiled.

"We'll be in touch."

The big guy on downstairs-lobby duty was in place, so talking my way through was out again. But then, I didn't plan on chatting to him. Ron and I approached, and he crossed his arms and made himself big, which was actually enormous, and very wide. But not wide enough. He didn't fill the whole hallway, so as Ron opened his mouth to speak and took the big unit's attention, I stepped around him and ran for the stairs. The big guy turned like he was part of the Carnival Line, and I was halfway up the stairs before he even reached the door. I ran up, three at a time, and figured I could do four if I got back into the beach running. I hit the door into the vacant top-floor reception and headed for Jenny's office. The big guy in the lobby must have been using all his energy to chase me up the stairs, because I expected him to call Finau and for the security boss to meet me in the hallway. But it didn't happen. I pushed open the doors to Jenny's office. She was standing by the window, Finau on the other side of her desk. Neither looked happy, but it was turning out to be that sort of day.

"What are you doing in here?" said Finau, striding to meet me in the middle of the room. I stopped before he got to me.

"We have business to discuss," I said, looking at Jenny.

"You have nothing here. Get out," said Finau. I could see the veins in his throat bulge, and I got the impression that he was about to become very unprofessional. Clearly he wasn't happy about us setting fire to his cousins. But Jenny stepped in.

"What are you doing here, Miami?" she said gently, like she was glad I had dropped in but wasn't sure why I had.

"Where do I start?"

"Start with this," said Ron, who had appeared behind me at the door. Clearly the elevator had gotten up the solitary floor faster than the big Tongan had on the stairs.

"Framing an employee for a crime. Fraud. Attempted murder. All of which runs afoul of the state of Florida's requirement for holders of gaming licenses to be of high moral character. Among other things."

It was a pretty good summation of things, all in all. I turned to Jenny.

"What he said."

Jenny smiled and came around the desk. "What do you think is happening here, Miami?"

Suddenly I didn't see her looking so great in a burlap sack. More in orange coveralls, and they really weren't her color.

"You're in some serious trouble here, Jenny."

"I don't think so, Miami. You got a lot of ideas in your head, from where I don't know. But no proof of anything. So, as a friend, I caution you to not spread your lies, lest someone sue you into the ground."

The last three words were a tad unnecessary, and not a bit mean-spirited. I had nothing to say in return, so I said nothing. I just held up my phone and hit the speaker. Jenny's recorded voice filled the office.

. . . it isn't going anywhere near a court room. We have gotten rid of Julio, and we will make a plan for Mr. Jones . . .

I tapped the screen with my thumb and let my name hang in the air. For a moment I saw Jenny's facade crack, but she regrouped fast.

"Miami, you are dealing with things of which you have no understanding."

"Sorry toots, but I'm not buying it," I said, doing my best gumshoe impersonation. "You are in it up to your pretty little armpits, and I'm taking you down." I turned to Finau. "You too."

Finau snarled. "You might have her, but you got nothing on me."

Again I lifted my phone and opened the app and hit the button. It was a pretty cool device, and added a good bit of drama. Now Stubbs' voice came out of the speaker.

. . . We need to talk, about Jones.

Then Finau:

Not now. I'm on it. He's deader than dead . . .

Finau didn't lose the snarl, and for a moment I thought he might pick me up and throw me through the window, but he didn't. He looked at me, he looked at Jenny, he looked at Ron.

Then he ran.

CHAPTER THIRTY—NINE

Finau played rugby as a younger man. I could see it in the burst of speed, I could see it in the way he ran, I could see it in the way he laid a stiff arm on Ron, driving his meaty paw into Ron's chest. Ron went flying, literally. His feet left the ground, and his arms flapped at his side, but he didn't have any upward thrust so it was all for naught, and he dropped onto his back, crashing into the carpet as Finau powered away. I ran forward to Ron.

"You all right?" I said.

Ron cocked an eyebrow and coughed. "Did I get him?" he asked, smiling.

"You slowed him down. Will that do?"

"Go get him, tiger."

I nodded and pushed off like a sprinter, headed for the fire stairs door that was edging closed. I hit the door at pace and leaped down the stairs four or five at a time, lucky not to break an ankle on the turn, and burst out into the lobby. The big unit who patrolled that area was waiting. I assumed Finau had given him instructions to stop me, because that's what he tried to do. He lunged with a hefty fist that would have ended up somewhere in the middle of my brain, but didn't. He was strong but slow, and I dodged him easily. He was ready for me to try sidestepping him again, this time spreading his legs to provide better sideways movement. I didn't have time to negotiate or show him the error of his ways, and his move provided me with the tactical advantage. He outmatched me physically in every area, except one. So I lined him up, and like a punter with two seconds on the clock, I kicked for the game winner. I connected right between his balls and butt bone, and with a pretty nasty crack, he collapsed. Had he been standing properly, I would never have gotten past his chunky thighs, but that's the rub of the green. I vaulted over him and dashed out onto the casino floor.

The place was quiet as usual, and I dodged between the card tables with ease. Problem was, I wasn't sure where Finau had gone. The big guy lying in the hallway with his hand on his crotch had slowed me down enough. Then I saw Roto. He was running out of the jai alai fronton and caught my eye.

"Señor Miami!" he yelled, pointing into the fronton.

I sprinted to him, and together we ran into the fronton. The other pelotari were gathered around, the game having been stopped by a big Tongan running through.

"He went to the back," said one of the pelotari, whose name escaped me. In their polo playing shirts they all looked the same to me.

"We have to get him," I yelled at Roto. "He's the one who tried to kill you."

Roto yelled a command, something in Spanish, and the pelotari started moving. I didn't wait to see what they were up to. I charged for the door.

I burst out into the dull sunlight, gravel crunching underfoot, the drone of the freeway omnipresent. Scanning the parking lot, I saw no movement. Then the door thrust open behind me and a troop of jai alai players marched out. They lined up in formation, like an artillery battalion, each man having strapped on their cesta—the long basket they used for jai alai.

"There." One of the players pointed, using his cesta to direct our attention. About a hundred yards out, Finau stood up from behind a car and made a break for his own vehicle. He had to give up his cover to do it—the lot being as sparsely populated as ever. I watched Finau run away, frozen in spot. I couldn't get to him before he reached his car, and my car was parked even further away. He was going to get away.

Then Roto stepped up and yelled.

"Fire!"

The line of pelotari loaded up their cestas with pelotas, the hard balls that were designed to smash against a granite wall, and they swung and thrust their right arms with the ferocity of a fastball pitcher, shooting balls into the air like mini missiles. The power behind the throws was awesome, and I realized why these guys were so athletic-looking and came off the court covered in sweat. It was harder than it looked. But the pelotari were pros.

The first pelota exploded a shower of gravel in front of Finau, making him slow down, not sure if he was being shot at. The second pelota hit a car just behind him with a tremendous metallic crack, leaving a huge divot in the trunk. Then the sky fell. Hard, goat skin-covered balls dropped from the sky at an alarming velocity, smashing around and into Finau. He was hit in the stomach by a low-slung shot that nearly launched him off his feet, then one cracked into his right shin, dropping him to his knees. I had to think that would smart, if not break bone. Several more shots hit him in the chest and shoulders, dropping him fully to the ground. There was a hiatus, where the sky cleared and the battery stopped. Finau picked himself up onto his hands and knees, looking my way. He smiled. He had withstood our assault, and was out of here.

But the pelotari were not done. Someone had dragged out a bag of pelotas, and the boys reloaded. Again, like a row of slingshots they thrust the pelota bombs across the parking lot, and as the sky filled with the hard balls once more, I saw Finau lose his smile. The jai alai boys must have found their range on the first round, because the second volley was targeted with laser-like accuracy. The pelotas rained down on Finau, onto his chest and shoulders and head, knocking him senseless. As the pelotari finished their throws, we ran forward in formation, like a forwarding army, toward Finau. I wasn't wearing a cumbersome basket on one arm, so I got to him first. He was out cold, which was a good thing because he looked like a sleeping bear. The rest of the guys arrived, and they wasted no time trussing him up like a Thanksgiving turkey, using the long reeds that were used to create the cestas.

The Palm Beach County Judicial Complex was on Gun Club Road, not too far from us, and although this was technically police territory, I called the number I had on speed dial in my phone.

"Palm Beach Sheriff's Office, how may I direct your call?"

"Is that Lucy?" I said, recognizing the voice as one of the civilian reception staff at the office.

"Who am I speaking to?"

"Lucy, this is Miami Jones."

"Miami, how are you?" she said.

"So-so, Luce. I've got a guy at the West Palm Jai Alai who tried to kill one of the players."

"Are you safe?"

"He's unconscious right now, but some proper cuffs pretty soon would be nice."

"I'll get a patrol car out to you right now."

I left the pelotari to guard Finau and jogged back into the fronton, past the jai alai court and onto the gaming floor. The big unit I had kicked in the coccyx was gone, so I ran up the stairs, one at a time. I really needed to get

into shape. I found Ron sitting against the doorjamb of
Jenny's office, where I had left him.

"Having a day off?" I said.

"Do I have a fruity drink in my hand?"

"No," I said.

"Then not a day off." Ron looked into the office, and
then back at me. "She kicked me, Miami. Kicked me. In
the face. I'm lucky I didn't lose an eye."

"Where is she, Ron?"

"She ran. She's gone. And I'm here to tell you, she's
not nearly as nice as you think she is."

I nodded.

I had managed to get to that conclusion all by myself.

CHAPTER FORTY

The question was, where would an out-of-towner go on the run? I helped Ron up, his injuries superficial but sure to grow into severe wounds the more he told the story, and we hotfooted it down to the rental car.

"What does she drive?" said Ron.

"What do you think? A convertible. Lexus, I think."

"Get the cops to put out a BOLO?"

"Not a bad idea, but we don't know the license plate and they're not going to stop every convertible Lexus in the Palm Beaches. That would annoy some very serious people."

We got in the car and I pulled out toward the exit with no idea where I was going. I headed right, thinking she might hit the freeway.

"Okay, let's think about this," said Ron. "Where would you go if you were on the run?"

"Easy. Longboard's. I could hide there for a month, beer included."

"All right, so let's assume Almondson isn't going to do that," he said.

"What about you, where would you go?" I said, pulling out onto I-95, moving for the sake of moving.

"Me? I'd head for the marina."

"The marina?"

"Yep. I'd grab the first boat I could and sail for the Bahamas."

"She's from New Jersey. Let's assume she doesn't know sailing and doesn't know where the Bahamas are. Where do you go?"

We both looked out the window at the same time, cruising along the freeway as a passenger jet dropped over our heads toward the airport.

Ron spun to look at me, but I was already looking at him. I glanced back at the road a split second too late, as we went zooming by the airport exit. I smashed on the brakes and skidded into the stopping lane. There was traffic behind me but not a lot, so I dropped the gear in reverse and hurtled backwards along the freeway. Horns were blaring, but I kept going, onto the island that separated the freeway from the off-ramp. I crunched the gear back into drive, and the little car screamed, and tires skidded and a minivan jumped on the brakes with full horn, just missing us. I screamed down the off-ramp, ignoring the light as I wrenched the car onto Belvedere Road.

As I drove, Ron got on my phone and called the last number again. He told the dispatcher who he was, and that he was with me, and he said that the other suspect was probably headed for PBI, and for them to call the airport cops.

"She's got patrols at the airport already, more on the way," said Ron. "Their guys on the ground are contacting airport police."

We pulled off Belvedere and onto the access road to the terminal. Palm Beach International Airport doesn't get the traffic of the bigger hubs in Lauderdale and Miami, but what it does get is plenty of lost octogenarians. We were met with a wall of slow-moving rental cars and forty-year-old Cadillacs. Cars were slowing to read the signs overhead, terminal directions and long-term parking and rental car return. One Caddie made their turn across three lanes, sans indicator. No one but me seemed to mind. I saw a guy in a hat take some eyeglasses from his wife and put them on, all without holding the steering wheel. I wondered how he had been reading the road signs up until that point.

We crawled up to the terminal, and I pulled into a white zone at a haphazard angle, and Ron and I jumped out and ran for the doors. A traffic cop called after us.

"You can't leave your vehicle. Loading and unloading only."

We didn't wait to chat about it. We ran into the departures level. There were people with suitcases on roller wheels everywhere. No one seemed to be where they wanted to be, because everyone was in motion. Which made it impossible to spot any one suspect. Ron slapped my chest and pointed to the departure board. I scanned the options. There was a flight to Westchester, New York, leaving in ten minutes.

"New York," I said. "Heading to home base?"

Ron shook his head.

"Three hours in the air. Cops could check the manifest and have a team waiting at the other end. I'd want to leave the country."

I was scanning the board again when a hand dropped on my shoulder.

"That your car parked like a drunk out there?" It was the traffic cop.

"Officer, my name is Miami Jones. We called in an attempted murder suspect possibly trying to flee via the airport. Did you get the call?"

He dropped his chin to the handset of his radio and called it in. It came back affirmative.

"Where is the suspect headed?"

"We don't know," I said. "Maybe the islands. Do you know when the next flight out is?"

"There," he pointed to the board. "Nassau. Departing in fifteen."

"Not long enough to get through security, is it?"

"It is if you're flying first class," he said.

I had no doubt that Jenny Almondson would fly up at the front of the plane. She was that kind of gal.

"Where?" I said.

The cop nodded and started jogging away, and Ron and I followed. We left the check-in kiosks and rows of luggage, and headed past a coffee shop toward the security line.

"She could be through," I said. The traffic cop stepped over to the TSA agent checking IDs, and gave her the lowdown. The agent nodded, and the cop turned to me.

"I'll walk the concourse, see if anyone fits your description. Pretty blond, you say?"

I nodded.

"That narrows it down," he said.

"In a black pinstripe business suit."

"Okay, not so many of them here."

The cop took off through the security cordon, and Ron and I decided to wander in opposite directions to see if we saw her. I headed back toward the check-in kiosks, rows of sad faces leaving Florida and returning to shoveling snow and frozen windshields and iced-up streets. I dashed back out to the road and scanned the traffic and the stopped vehicles. She might have gone to the long-term lot. It wouldn't have been as quick, but it would be more under the radar, and she probably didn't know we were this close. Assuming, of course, that she was at the airport at all. She could just as easily have stayed on I-95. Eighteen hours later she'd find herself crossing the George Washington Bridge into Manhattan. I turned away, doubting our logic now, but sure that this was the better play for the moment. If she was on the freeway, we had more time. I-95 was covered in CCTV cameras designed to read license plates, so if she was still in her Lexus, there was a chance we'd find her. Not so much if she landed in a foreign country. I wandered back inside and scanned the faces again, seeing nothing.

Then I froze.

Walking away from a first-class check-in desk was a black pinstripe suit, draped in blond hair. For a moment I hesitated, watching her walk. She had no luggage and walked with as much speed as high heels allowed without looking clumsy.

"Jenny," I called. My voice was swallowed in the white noise of people and movement and electronics. I took two steps toward a long trolley of luggage and gave it another go.

"Jenny!"

Heads turned in my direction. One of them was the blond in the pinstripes. She was frowning, not a great look for her, and her eyes scanned the crowd for the source. Then they locked on me. For a moment Jenny and I looked at each other across the humdrum of the terminal. Her face softened slightly, or that might just have been the light. Then she set her jaw.

"I told you, I'm not running a two-bit jai alai show forever," she said.

"What did Hoskin offer you?" I realized now that Danielle was right; teamwork was everything, and competitors were often better as partners.

Jenny shook her head. "Offer me?" She laughed but not because anything was funny. "He didn't offer me anything. You don't get it."

"Tell me. We can work it out," I said, not really believing the words spilling from my mouth.

Jenny stood erect, defiant to the end. "I don't need your help, Miami. I have all the help I need."

"You mean Hoskin? He's going to hang you out to dry."

"Hoskin doesn't tell my people what to do." Jenny glanced sideways, along the rows of check-in kiosks, and I saw her eye fix on something. I turned and saw what had her attention. Two airport cops were wandering across the concourse, on routine patrol. I looked back to Jenny. She looked at me.

Then she ran.

I had no idea what her thought process was at this point, but I guessed if the options were fight or flight, and you had chosen flight, you just kept running, come hell or high water, until you escaped or were caught.

She flicked off her shoes in a well-practiced move, then ran away in stockinged feet. I chased after her. There were more people around me, so I did a lot of bumping and got a lot of nasty looks, and by the time I had made it through the check-in area, she had put some distance between us. I took off faster now and saw Jenny running past the security line, toward the end of the terminal. She hit the skids for some reason and slid along the smooth floor, her stockings providing no traction. Then I saw why she had stopped. A team of airport police were ambling up the terminal, headed her way. They didn't seem to be looking for her, but seeing her skid to a stop and turn away piqued their interest. She ran from them, back toward me.

"Jenny," I said again, and again she skidded to a stop, right in front of the security line. She turned to the door out of the terminal, perhaps abandoning her flight plans, and started toward it. But it wasn't her lucky day. As she did, the doors slid open and four Palm Beach sheriff's deputies strode in. They, unlike the airport cops, were very much looking for Jenny. I saw her stiffen and freeze. I glanced back at the deputies and noticed one of them was different than the others. This one was a woman. She was making the uniform look a hell of a lot better than the guys. Her brown hair shone and her piercing eyes never left the suspect. I watched as Danielle pulled her sidearm from its holster. She pointed it at Jenny.

"Freeze," she said. Her colleagues joined in the chorus, then it was like rounds as the airport cops got in on the act and started yelling *Freeze* and *Police*.

Jenny panicked. It was a natural, understandable reaction. Freezing was the smart play, but she was in flight mode, and she turned and ran, her feet slipping on the plastic tile, pumping with limited effect, like the Road Runner building up momentum, then bursting away from the coyote. Jenny ran toward security, past the woman checking IDs. Once she hit the carpet she got traction and picked up speed, around the rope line that was herding travelers like cattle. She hurdled the final rope with impressive ease and dashed for the X-ray scanner. She hit the scanner and it burst to life, probably from coins or pens or her watch, and through she went. Somewhere deep down she had to know she was headed for a dead end, but where there's life, there's hope.

And then there was a large TSA agent. She was tasked with patting down female passengers and was watching as Jenny burst through the security scanner, setting the thing off. The TSA agent was not armed, but that didn't dissuade her. As Jenny stepped to run around her, the agent put her arm out straight and poleaxed her. The stiff arm coat-hangered her, right in the throat. Jenny's momentum kept her feet going, the lower half of her body flying straight under the agent's arm, but her upper half came to a violent and sudden stop. Jenny flipped, crashing onto her back, grabbing at her throat, and sucking for air.

The TSA agent's face did not change. She was passive, her face devoid of emotion, like there was no difference between patting down a traveler and almost decapitating a fugitive. The airport cops ran through the security cordon, weapons drawn, but their work had been done for them. Jenny Almondson wasn't going anywhere fast. Paramedics were called, and the deputies put their sidearms away. Danielle saw me and wandered over.

"You're home," I said.

"Yeah. Was hoping I'd catch you later."

I smiled. "Fair chance of that."

"Who's your girlfriend?" she asked, nodding toward the fallen Jenny Almondson.

"She's no . . . oh. She runs the casino where Desi made his bets. It's a long story."

"You can tell me over a fruity drink later."

"Deal."

Danielle smiled and turned back to her colleagues.

"Danielle," I said.

She looked back over her shoulder, and I almost had a cardiac arrest.

"It's good to have you home."

She nodded. "It's great to be home."

She winked and turned away, and I saw Ron wander up from the other end of the terminal.

"What'd I miss?" he asked, smiling.

We watched the paramedics load Jenny onto a gurney, and we saw a cop cuff her to it. The TSA agent who had downed her was relieved of duty in order to give a statement, and she asked if she was still on the clock. She said she wasn't giving no statement on her own time. She wandered through the security scanner, and it beeped. She was what you might call a large-boned woman, chocolate brown skin and a serious face.

"Nice job, ma'am," I said.

She shrugged.

I thought about Finau lying on the gravel back at the casino.

"Ma'am, do you mind if I ask you a question? Where are you from, originally?"

Her steely facade broke open, and she gave me the biggest, toothiest smile I'd ever seen. "Tonga," she said. "Have you been?"

"No, but I'm thinking I should go."

"You should, you'd love it. People are very nice there."

CHAPTER FORTY-ONE

The extraordinary general meeting of the Palm Beach
Town Council attracted a bigger crowd than normal. That
was an assumption on my part, given I'd never been to a
meeting before, but judging by the fact that the gallery
was standing-room only, it was an accurate one. Everyone
who was anyone on the island was there. News crews
gathered on the steps outside. It was a big deal,
considering the meeting was being held to decide to do
nothing.

The sole agenda item was the proposed resort
development and its gaming implications to the town and
the island. There was no doubt that the rich residents
wanted no part of it, and they had made their feelings
known to their elected officials. News had spread about
my beating at the hands of employees of Elroy Hoskin,
and although no charges had been filed, it had done
nothing for his reputation in Palm Beach. The meeting

had been called to quash the project before it even began. There were five speakers against the project and fifty others who wanted to take the microphone. No one, not even Elroy Hoskin, spoke in favor. Motions were passed, restricting building permits on classified buildings like the Colonial Hotel, and further amendments were passed regarding the issuance of new permits of large, non-residential projects. An ordinance was passed restricting the number of passengers that could board a vessel at the marina without a permit. I noted that the size of the vessel was not mentioned, for many of the resident's boats were bigger than the high-speed ferries Hoskin had proposed.

There was a lot of hushed talk and quiet back-slapping in the foyer of City Hall after the meeting. I saw Elroy Hoskin looking too relaxed, as if nothing affected him. I chatted with my friend Jimmy Tigerfoot, who I had invited to the meeting with the promise of a stone crab feed with beers after. Hoskin made his way across the room and stopped by me.

"Consider your services terminated, Jones," he said.

"I never considered them engaged, but okay. Say, have you met my good friend? Jimmy Tigerfoot."

Jimmy shook hands with Hoskin, and Hoskin offered a tight smile.

"Jimmy's a member of the Seminole tribe. Isn't that right, Jimmy?"

Jimmy nodded and beamed. "That's right."

Hoskin lost the smile. He looked like he'd eaten a bad pickle. "You're a riot, Jones. But I built a paradise in the Nevada desert. I can outwait these Indians."

Jimmy gave him a wink. "We been waiting centuries," he said. "So no problems. Bring it on."

"I hear Myrtle Beach is nice this time of year," I offered.

"You think you're clever, but you have no idea what is going on here," snarled Hoskin.

He turned and walked away from us, talking to an aide.

"Get me a report on Myrtle Beach," he said.

Jimmy looked at me, and we both laughed.

"You've made Jackie Bass a very happy man, doing all this," said Jimmy.

"Things were going all right for Jackie and the tribe, regardless. The governor has more or less confirmed a new Compact. This was just the icing on the cake." I pulled out my wallet and found the gaming credit Jackie Bass had given me. "Maybe you can give this back to Jackie for me?"

Jimmy shook his head. "Jackie don't need it. Next time you're down, you put it on red. You win, you do something good with it."

That sounded like a fair plan to me.

We got out into the cool evening, the steps of City Hall as busy as the foyer. News crews were trawling for familiar faces, for comment. Most of the residents of the island eschewed publicity. Elroy Hoskin was clearly no resident of Palm Beach. He stopped in the lights of the cameras and waited patiently as the news crews moved their equipment into position.

"Ladies and gentlemen, of course I am disappointed in the proceedings this evening. I don't see this as an attack on our proposed resort, but rather on all development in the Palm Beaches. It remains to be seen if the State courts agree with the legality of these decisions."

"So you plan to sue?" said a reporter.

"I am keeping all options open at this time. But as I have said all along, we see a need, a desire, for more entertainment in this part of South Florida. Unlike the town council of Palm Beach, I don't wish to see those jobs and that economic benefit leaving the area. We believe we have an exciting proposal to put forward soon, one that has always been part of my dream for the Palm Beaches, and one that will benefit all people in the area, especially in West Palm Beach, where these jobs are so vitally needed."

Another reporter called out. "What do you say then to the vote tonight by the West Palm Beach City Commission to put a moratorium on any further gaming permits for a minimum of five years?"

Hoskin frowned and glanced at his minders. "I am aware of no commission meeting tonight," he said.

The reporter continued. "A special meeting was called by the mayor and the president of the commission. Essentially, they have banned further gaming in the city and reaffirmed the status of the pari-mutuels as requiring their sports components. How does this affect your plan?"

I watched Hoskin closely. He was a pro, that was for sure. He held himself together but I saw the stress lines crack open around his eyes. When I had met the mayor of West Palm at Hoskin's party, I had sown the seed that Hoskin was playing off the island against West Palm, and that he never intended to develop in Palm Beach, but rather use that threat to get influential backing to move the project onto the mainland. The mayor had scoffed but pulled at the collar of his tuxedo all the same. There is nothing the city of West Palm Beach hates more than being considered second fiddle to Palm Beach. They have a real complex about it. So when I dumped the tapes on his desk that morning, he jumped into action. While Hoskin was festering his plan on the island, supposedly watching it go down in flames in Palm Beach, it was actually burning to the ground in West Palm.

"I have no further comment at this time. Thank you," said Hoskin, waving to the bright lights like he was walking the red carpet at the Oscars. He stepped away from the media melee, and his entourage pushed its way down the steps. Eric Edwards met Hoskin at the bottom of the steps. I had primed Eric with details of the threats to the pelotari and my beating in Palm Beach.

"Sir, I am State Attorney Eric Edwards. Can I have a word about alleged death threats to employees of a West

Palm Beach gaming establishment, and the assault of a local resident?"

A guy I assumed to be Hoskin's attorney stepped forward.

"Are you out of your mind?" he hissed. "You can't do this here."

Eric smiled. "Perhaps at the Hall of Justice then? I have a patrol car waiting."

The attorney looked like he was about to pop a valve. Hoskin pushed him away and stood chest to chest with Edwards.

"Edwards," said Hoskin. "You're the fellow who is looking to run for office."

"I've never said anything like that," gushed Eric.

"A campaign needs solid support," said Hoskin. "Why don't we talk about all these matters in my car?" he said, pointing to the stretch limo that pulled up with impressive timing.

Eric looked at the limo and then back at Hoskin. Hoskin smiled.

"Why not?" said Eric, getting into the car.

I crossed my arms and smiled. Some things never change.

CHAPTER FORTY-TWO

Ron and I stood by the smoldering rubble. What had been a well-built, if old and ugly building, now looked like ground zero. The heat had been so intense prior to the fire department's arrival that the bones of the structure had collapsed, toppling the building onto itself. The fire chief on the scene wandered over to us.

"Miami," said the chief.

I nodded to him. I had subbed occasionally as a batter on the fire department's softball team.

"You know this place?" he said.

"Was a two-story office, wasn't it?" I said.

He nodded.

"Yeah, I mean you know the owner?"

"Nah, the owner I don't know. But the tenant was an illegal bookmaker. Used to take off-course bets down at the jai alai."

He turned, and we all watched nothing happening. I cast my mind back to my only visit to this place, when Lucas and I had confronted the bookie who had ultimately taken the bets from Desi. Now his entire operation lay in a hot pyre.

"Anyone in there?" I said.

"Not that we can tell. What brings you guys out here?" said the chief.

"Ron heard it on the radio, and we'd been here recently, so . . . "

"You know this bookie, then?"

"Not well. We've just wrapped up a case that involved the jai alai and we came into contact with this dirtbag."

The chief frowned. "You guys can provide alibis for last night, right?"

"What time?" I asked.

"Say, between eight and nine."

The timing couldn't have been any more perfect, and I got the feeling that was the point. I looked at Ron.

"We were both at the Palm Beach Council meeting," said Ron.

"Someone vouch for that?"

Ron shrugged. "About half the island, I'd say. Why?"

"This was a professional job, all right," said the chief.

"How so?" I said.

"Whoever did this, they really knew their stuff. The investigation will tell us more, but to my eye, the spine of the fire was specifically designed to destabilize the structure in such a way that it collapsed, but collapsed into that vacant block."

We looked at the vacant lot where about a third of the building now lay.

"It's pretty rare that the adjoining building is unharmed, but apart from a little water damage, that's the case," he said, pointing at the building on the other side, standing beside its fallen brother.

"And the accelerant," continued the chief. "Not sure what it was yet, but it was hot. Maybe a metallic compound. Either way, it was done in such a way that the structural damage was complete before there were any signs of fire on the outside. So by the time we got here, it was already all over. Our hoses just helped the building collapse." The chief turned to me. "But don't quote me on that," he smiled.

The fire department had a truck on the scene, but it was mainly to keep people away. The blaze had burned itself out, but they were waiting for the whole thing to cool down before checking it further.

"So you think this guy has enemies," said the chief, "or money problems?"

"I'd guess both," I said. "But he definitely looked like a man with money worries."

A fire investigator walked over to us in a crisp white shirt.

"Chief, we just got a call from the PD. They have a name on a tenant. It's a company called Trix Leisure Ltd.

Seems they just got a call out to a storage locker rented in that same name, signed by someone called Barrett."

The chief looked at me.

"You know that name?"

I nodded.

"That's the bookie."

The chief turned back to his man and told him to continue.

"Well, the night guard reported suspicious activity early this morning. Get this. Locker is full of documents, ledgers, cash."

"You don't say?" said the chief.

"And one more thing. The locker also contained accelerant, explosives, the lot. PD reckons enough to recreate Krakatoa."

The chief glanced at us and nodded. "Excuse me, gents. I've got work to do."

We watched him walk away with his investigator, then we got back in the car. I sat without starting the engine.

"You seen Lucas?" said Ron.

I shook my head slowly.

"Not since he lit a fire under some Tongans."

"Spoken to him?"

I shook my head again. "Left a voicemail for him, though. To tell him the bookie's van was back in business, and we'd had no effect."

Ron looked out the window at the collapsed building and spoke softly, as if to himself.

"I'd say that was an effect."

CHAPTER FORTY—THREE

There are few places I love more than the fairy-lit courtyard at Longboard Kelly's on a mild winter's night. The colored light threw a festive glow over the space, and for the first time in a long time I felt as good as I could remember. I clinked beers with Ron.

"Another job well done, more or less," I said.

"One for the good guys," said Ron.

Then I swiveled on my barstool and clinked my beer with Danielle's vodka tonic.

"Great to have you back," I said.

She smiled. "Great to be had."

We sipped our drinks and surveyed the courtyard. Most of the tables were occupied and there was a buzz in the air.

"So what happened to Desi?" said Danielle.

"He's back with his uncle, and his uncle has his money, so he can't do anything silly with it. Hopefully soon he gets enough to get his family over here."

Danielle caught the look in my eye and smiled. "You want to do something, don't you?" she said.

"I went down to the Hard Rock and put the gaming credit Jackie Bass gave me on red."

"Okay."

"And it came up red. Three times."

"Nice for you."

"I was thinking about getting a television."

"What would you do with a television?"

"There is that. Well, since I don't need the cash . . ." I said.

"I love you," said Danielle. "I don't pretend to understand you, but I do love you."

"Right back at ya," I said. I turned to Ron. "I love you, too, buddy."

"Oh, I know that. So you really don't need to say it. Really."

We laughed and sipped our drinks.

"So here's the gap in the story," said Danielle. "I don't get how you made the leap from that witch Almondson to Hoskin and back?"

"Witch?" I said.

"She was after you, boyo. She got off easy, getting slugged by the TSA. Just saying."

"Oh-kay. She made the mistake of mentioning Hoskin to Stubbs. We got it on tape. So we knew there was a link. As for what that link was, you actually gave me the idea," I said.

"Me?" she smiled. "See, I'm solving cases, and I'm not even here. Go on."

"Well, you were talking about how the departments didn't fight each other, even though that was the popular view. That cooperation was everything. And it got me thinking. We kept seeing all these players as adversaries. But sometimes adversaries make convenient bedfellows. I kept thinking that for an astute guy, Hoskin had really misread his target market. But he hadn't. It was a ploy. He made a big ruckus about Palm Beach, knowing the residents would raise hell. He then planned to use their influence in the capital to convince the state to allow him his dreaded resort, but with the trade-off that it was built anywhere but Palm Beach."

"But why West Palm?" she said.

"At his big presentation he kept saying that the gamblers—and he meant the low-rent, non-Palm Beach types—would be essentially kept away at another facility. Limos could take the jet set there, but he never said where. And Sally reminded me that the politicians didn't want to open more gaming locations."

I took a sip and continued. "So I started thinking, what if they didn't? What if they cooperated? Hoskin does it. He owns all his Las Vegas properties outright, but he has joint ventures all over, like Macau and Australia. So why not join with the New York outfit who has a pari-mutuel license here already, and would be better off with a smaller piece of a much bigger pie?"

"But the jai alai license has to keep jai alai, not kill it," said Ron.

"Yeah, that was the wrench in the works. But Sal and Eric both said the state liked the imagery of it. But if it was failing, seen to be killing jobs, then there would be incentive to change that law."

"They wanted to kill jai alai so they could show it was killing jobs?" said Danielle.

"Exactly. They needed that imagery the politicians so loved to turn ugly. Julio and his guys were putting a wrench in that plan. But then Stubbs of all people put the nail in the coffin. And when I caught up with Jenn—" I looked at Danielle and stopped, then, "Ms. Almondson, at the airport, she told me she didn't need Hoskin, that she had her own people. Then the pieces started to fit."

I finished my beer and nodded to Muriel for another round.

"I found it odd that she was at Hoskin's party, and she was surprised I was there. She claimed that you never knew where you might end up. But she knew, because her New York bosses were already working with Hoskin. When she said she might work for one casino today and another tomorrow, I thought she meant she might defect to Hoskin's organization. But she was talking about her New York organization. She was the point man, or point woman, for the New Yorkers' partnership with Hoskin. They planned to kill the pari-mutuel and set up a Vegas-style casino, with no additional gambling license required. They just needed to paint the proper picture for the politicians. All she had to do was show jai alai as unpopular and corrupt, like it was a cancer on the city, killing jobs, and her reward would be to run the joint-venture resort. So when she linked Hoskin to her New York bosses, I just took a copy of Stubbs's tape to our esteemed mayor. Once he learned that Hoskin and New York were teaming up, and that the Vegas mogul was playing the city of West Palm for chumps, he got, well, indignant. It was as fired up as I've ever seen him. They convened the meeting last minute to ensure Hoskin couldn't be there, and they nailed him."

Danielle nodded thanks to Muriel for her new drink and turned to me, straw in mouth. "What did Eric say? Will Hoskin go down?"

I laughed. "I think it's more likely that he'll end up a donor to Eric's campaign, but at least he won't be doing business here."

"Lot of jobs gone, though," said Danielle.

"But if what the mayor says is right, the net effect of jobs might have close to zero, anyway," I said.

"And without a lot of extra baggage those big casinos bring," said Ron.

"Guys," I said.

Danielle said amen to that and leaned around me to clink drinks with Ron.

"Ah, guys," I said, again, this time slapping Danielle's shoulder.

"You asked what happened to Desi . . ."

Danielle frowned in her seat, then spun around and smiled.

Desi stood at the entrance to the Longboard's courtyard. But this time he wasn't alone. His uncle was there, and his aunt and cousin. And another man and woman, with two girls I didn't know.

"Come in," I said, waving them toward us and getting off my stool.

Danielle slipped down from her own stool.

"Hi, Desi," she smiled.

Desi shuffled his feet, then the man I didn't know gave him a light tap behind the ear, and the boy shuffled over to Danielle. He stood before her and handed her a sweater. My Oakland A's sweater. Then the kid broke out into a huge grin and launched into a full-force hug. Danielle beamed.

Desi's uncle spoke to me.

"Your office said you would be here. We wanted to say thank you."

I didn't think I'd done that much. The thing with the big Boston guys, and the van and the bookies, that was nothing they ever need know about. But as Lenny always said: *give praise liberally and take it with grace.*

"Thanks," I said. "You're welcome. I'm sorry, I don't know your friends."

Desi's uncle did a double take and then gave an embarrassed grin. "I am sorry. This is not my friend. This is my brother-in-law. Desi's father."

I frowned. "I thought Desi's father was in Cuba."

"Yes, he was."

"So how is he here now? You got the money?"

Desi's uncle spoke in Spanish, and the family all laughed. Then he spoke to me.

"We did not spend money. Mr. Lucas went and got him. He got all of Desi's family."

"From Cuba?" I almost shouted, but caught myself.

"Si. From Veradero. He go in a big fast boat and collected them all. He is a very brave man."

I fell back onto my stool and looked at Ron. Lucas had disappeared, saying he had a boat delivery to do. It seemed, however, that it was more of a pickup. I could just see him taking the pick of the fast boats in the marina and sneaking off across the straits. It was Lucas all over.

I looked to Desi's father and offered my hand.

"*Bienvenido a Estados Unidos*," I said.

He smiled, the kind of smile you only see on those rare days, when someone is given a lifetime's worth of Christmases all in one go.

CHAPTER FORTY—FOUR

Danielle didn't take her eyes off the water as I filled her wine glass. She was as happy as a pig in something that would make a pig very happy. Desi's family had stayed a while at Longboard's, but already not wishing to overstay their welcome, bade us goodnight after extending an invitation for a pre-Christmas party at a park near Los Piños. Danielle had talked to the boy and his sisters the whole time and had been smiling ever since.

"You're a long way away," I said.

She looked over to me as I sat on my lounger. "Sorry, just thinking."

"About?"

"Everything. My job. Desi." She glanced at me. "You."

"What about me?"

"Sorry I've been distant," she said. "I don't know what happened to me."

"I do."

She sipped her wine. "Oh, oracle, do share."

"You got shot."

"There was that."

"And that dented your confidence. Worse still, it dented your confidence in me. And that made me . . . I don't know. Pull away. I thought I was just comfortable. Happy to get fat and lazy. But it wasn't that. I was playing it safe."

"Go on," she said.

"I guess I didn't want to take risks when it came to you, because taking risks meant I could lose you. But it wasn't until you were away that I realized playing it safe might mean losing you, too."

Danielle nodded. "I felt that, you know," she said. "Like we've been drifting. Drifting together and drifting apart. But while I was away, it was like a lightning bolt. Like I'm not doing myself justice, not giving it my all. And all of a sudden, these important people gave me the time of day and valued me. And I realized that the problem wasn't that people didn't value me before, it was that I wasn't putting enough value on myself. That changes. Today."

I smiled. "Glad to hear it."

"You too," she said, getting fired up now. "I agree with what you are saying. So cut the crap. You are who you are. And I fell in love with that guy. Yeah, I got shot. And you're right, that hit me harder than I wanted to admit. But I know you didn't do that. And you need to know that, too. Bad guys did that. And there are always bad guys. And for whatever reason, we are the people to stop them. So cut the crap."

I had nothing to say to that, so I said nothing.

"And one more thing. Ron says you're looking at replacing the Escape with a minivan."

"Ron says a lot of things."

"No minivan. Are you kidding me? The Miami Jones does not drive a minivan."

"I agree. But just to be clear, what does the Miami Jones drive?"

"Not a minivan."

"A Ford Escape hybrid?"

Danielle screwed her nose up.

"I was looking at a Porsche Boxster," I said.

"A Porsche? Can you afford that?"

"A used one. A few miles on the clock, but plenty to go."

Danielle thought about that for a second. "Convertible?" she said.

"Of course."

"Can I drive it on weekends?"

"*Mi coche, su coche.*"

Danielle nodded. "A Porsche," she said again. "That could work."

I was already liking this cutting the crap business. I went with it.

"More wine?"

She shook her head. "No, thanks. Have to run in the morning."

"You do?"

"And you. Don't think I don't see that muffin top."

"It's more like a baby cupcake."

"Pfft."

"Okay, then. A run. What's the bet?" I asked.

"City Beach to the State Park and back. Loser pays. Since you just won some money you don't need."

"Loser pays for what?"

She didn't look at me, but I could see the twinkle in her eye.

"A vacation to Jamaica."

GET YOUR NEXT BOOK FREE

Hearing from you, my readers, is one of the the best things about being a writer. If you want to sign up to my mailing list, we'll not only be able to keep in touch, but you can also get an exclusive ebook, the Miami Jones novel Three Strikes, as well as occasional pre-release reads, and other goodies that are only available to my list friends.

Join Now:
http://www.ajstewartbooks.com/reader

ACKNOWLEDGEMENTS

Thanks, as always, to all my readers who send me feedback. A huge thanks to Constance Renfrow and Beth Balmanno for their editorial expertise; all the beta readers, especially Heather, Andrew, Maria, and Lauren; and the folks at the Starbucks in Ralph's of Sherman Oaks, where this book was partially written between ice coffees over a very hot valley summer. These books don't happen in isolation, so thank you. Any and all errors are mine, especially but not limited to my lifelong love of the Richmond Tigers. That's just heartbreak, right there.

If you're looking for it, there is no Jai Alai fronton in West Palm Beach anymore. Hey, it's fiction, so I made it up. There are (currently) Jai Alai frontons in Dania Beach, Fort Pierce, and Miami among others. I say currently because everything regarding the pari-mutuel system is true, and Jai Alai in South Florida is an endangered species. To see video of what the game looks like, and learn more about the fate of this unique sport, visit www.ajstewartbooks.com/jai-alai.

ABOUT THE AUTHOR

A.J. Stewart has lived in so many places it feels like he has a home team in every game he sees. Which explains why his wife begins any sports telecast with "who are we going for today?" A.J. and his family currently spend their time in Los Angeles and South Florida, but stay tuned, anything could happen.

You can find AJ online at www.ajstewartbooks.com, connect on Twitter @The_AJStewart or Facebook facebook.com/TheAJStewart.

Made in the USA
Middletown, DE
19 April 2021